Asimov's
Extraterrestrials

D1238668

In this series

Asimov's Extraterrestrials

Edited by Isaac Asimov, Martin Greenberg and Charles Waugh

DRAGON
GRAFTON BOOKS
A Division of the Collins Publishing Group

LONDON GLASGOW
TORONTO SYDNEY AUCKLAND

Dragon
Grafton Books
A Division of the Collins Publishing Group
8 Grafton Street, London W1X 3LA

First published in Great Britain by
Dragon Books 1986

First published in USA by Harper & Row,
Publishers, Inc., New York, 1984

British Library Cataloguing in Publication Data

[Young extraterrestrials]. Asimov's extraterrestrials.
   1. Children's stories, English   2. Science fiction, English
   I. Asimov, Isaac   II. Greenberg, Martin Harry
   III. Waugh, Charles G.
   823'.0876'089282[J]   PZ5

ISBN 0-583-30986-0

Printed and bound in Great Britain by
Collins, Glasgow

Set in Times

To Dr Janet O. Jeppson, Sally Greenberg and
Carol-Lynn Rôssel Waugh
Women all talented in their own right

Acknowledgements

'Doorstep' by Keith Laumer. Copyright © 1961 by Galaxy
Publishing Corporation. Reprinted by permission of Richard
Curtis Associates, Inc.

'In the Jaws of Danger' by Piers Anthony. Copyright © 1967 by
Galaxy Publishing Corporation. Reprinted by permission of
Kirby McCauley, Ltd.

'The Witness' by Eric Frank Russell. Copyright 1951 by Palmer
Publications, Inc., copyright renewed. Reprinted by permission
of the author's Estate and the agents for the Estate, Scott
Meredith Literary Agency, Inc., 845 Third Avenue, New York,
New York 10022.

'The Mississippi Saucer' by Frank B. Long. Copyright 1951 by
Short Stories, Inc. Reprinted by permission of Kirby McCauley,
Ltd.

'Primary Education of the Camiroi' by R. A. Lafferty. Copyright
© 1966, 1970 by R. A. Lafferty. Reprinted by permission of the
author and the author's agent, Virginia Kidd.

'Tween' by J. F. Bone. Copyright © 1978 by Ultimate Publishing
Company, Inc. Reprinted by permission of the author and the
author's agents, Scott Meredith Literary Agency, Inc., 845 Third
Avenue, New York, New York 10022.

'Zoo' by Edward D. Hoch. Copyright © 1958 by King-Size
Publications, Inc. Reprinted by permission of the author.

'Subcommittee' by Zenna Henderson. Copyright © 1962 by
Mercury Press, Inc. Reprinted by permission of Curtis Brown
Associates, Ltd.

'Keyhole' by Murray Leinster. Copyright 1951 by Standard
Magazines, Inc. Reprinted by permission of the author and the
author's agents, Scott Meredith Literary Agency, Inc., 845 Third
Avenue, New York, New York 10022.

'Kindergarten' by James Gunn. Copyright © 1970 by Universal
Publishing & Distributing Corporation. First published in Galaxy
Science Fiction, April 1970.

Contents

Introduction

We don't actually know if there are any extraterrestrials. As of now, there is only one world—only one—on which we know there is any life at all, let alone intelligent life, and that is Earth.

As far as our solar system is concerned, we have had nothing but disappointment. The Moon is too small to possess any noticeable air or water. Once astronauts landed there, and brought back Moon rocks, it became absolutely certain that there was no life on it, and never had been.

A pair of Viking probes landed on Mars in 1976, and the information they sent back seems to show there is no life on Mars, either. Mercury and Venus are far too hot for life, and the worlds beyond Mars are too cold. Some people speculate about possible odd forms of life in Jupiter's upper atmosphere or on its satellite Europa, which may have liquid water under an icy glacier that covers its entire surface. Could Saturn's satellite Titan, which has a thick atmosphere of nitrogen and methane, have some sort of life form? There are only the slimmest possibilities of this, however, and the chance that such life would be *intelligent* is far slimmer still.

But our Sun is only one star in a galaxy that contains somewhere between 200 and 300 billion stars all together; and our galaxy is only one of about 100 billion in the universe. If the planets that circle the Sun include only one world with life, what about the planets that circle the 10,000,000,000,000,000,000,000 other stars in the universe?

Well, we don't know. The stars are so far away that we can't study their neighborhoods in detail. We can't actually see the planets that circle them, and we don't even know if the other stars have any planets in the first place.

All we can do is speculate. Most astronomers have indeed done this and wondered whether there is life on other worlds and whether intelligent life might exist outside Earth. We might divide such astronomers into optimists and pessimists.

The optimists feel that all, or nearly all, stars do have planetary systems. Current theories are that stars form out of huge swirling masses of gas and dust, and in the process, small quantities of matter on the outskirts gather together and form planets even while the main body forms a huge star. In 1983, a telescope in orbit, one designed to study infrared radiation, detected a swirling mass of particles around the bright star Vega. It looked as though a planetary system was in the process of formation, which seems to increase the chances that planetary systems are the rule.

If that is so, astronomers can try to estimate how many stars will exist long enough to allow complex life forms to evolve on their planets, and will be large enough to supply enough energy, and won't be situated in places where there will be too high a level of dangerous radiation, and so on.

Counting just those stars that are of the right type, they then estimate how many planets of those stars are likely to be large enough to hold an atmosphere and ocean, but not so large that they'll hold the wrong kind; how many planets will be at just the right temperature, and be in just the right orbit, and so on.

Optimistic astronomers feel that quite a few stars could be just right, and that quite a few planets could be right, too, so there might be billions of life-bearing planets in our galaxy alone—and billions of billions in the entire universe.

Even if that is so, how many of all those life-bearing planets will carry *intelligent* life forms? Optimistic astronomers feel that, given enough time, intelligence is sure to evolve, and they are ready to assume that there may be millions of extra-terrestrial intelligences distributed here and there in our galaxy alone.

Pessimistic astronomers, however, are not at all sure that every star has a planetary system. They argue that the more we study the universe, the more it seems to be a violent place, full of collapsing stars, exploding stars, black holes, and deadly radiation, so there are very few places where life could safely develop.

Furthermore, they feel that for a planet to be suitable for life, it would have to possess so many just-right properties that it is very unlikely for any planet to have them all. Earth does have them, but that may be an incredible fluke, and there couldn't be many planets like it anywhere. Moreover, they feel that it is not easy for life to form even on a suitable planet, while the chances for intelligence to develop would be more unlikely still. They are ready to argue that the chances are we are the only intelligent life form anywhere in the galaxy, and that there may not be very many in other galaxies either.

Either way it's a speculation and there is no way whatsoever (so far) of deciding whether the optimists or the pessimists are correct, or whether the truth lies somewhere in between.

The optimists say that we ought to set up elaborate radio telescopes to try to detect signals from other intelligences, since the chances are that we would find some, and that our view of the universe would be completely changed as a result. The pessimists say that would be a waste of billions of dollars, for if there are other intelligences out in space, why haven't *they* reached us?

The optimists say that they may be just too far away to make the trip worthwhile, and that they are trying to reach us instead by radio signals, which we should look for. And so the argument goes on.

However there are two things we can be certain of:

1) If there are extraterrestrial intelligences, then stories about them could be very exciting.

2) If there are extraterrestrial intelligences, then they must certainly have children, and stories about *them* could be even more exciting.

This anthology of eleven stories about young extraterrestrials proves this point.

Keith Laumer

Doorstep

U.F.O.'s are commonly called saucers.
However, their shapes also resemble eggs.

Steadying his elbow on the kitchen table serving as desk, Brigadier General Straut leveled his binoculars and stared out through the second-floor window of the farmhouse at the bulky object lying canted at the edge of the woodlot. He watched the figures moving over and around the gray mass, then flipped the lever on the field telephone at his elbow.

"How are your boys doing, Major?"

"General, since that box this morning—"

"I know all about the box, Bill. So does Washington by now. What have you got that's new?"

"Sir, I haven't got anything to report yet. I have four crews on it, and she still looks impervious as hell."

"Still getting the sounds from inside?"

"Intermittently, General."

"I'm giving you one more hour, Major. I want that thing cracked."

The general dropped the phone back on its cradle and peeled the cellophane from a cigar absently. He had moved fast, he reflected, after the State Police notified him at nine forty-one last night. He had his men on the spot, the area evacuated of civilians, and a preliminary report on its way to Washington by midnight. At two thirty-six, they had discovered the four-inch cube lying on the ground fifteen feet from the huge object—missile, capsule, bomb—whatever it was. But now— several hours later—nothing new.

The field phone jangled. Straut grabbed it up.

"General, we've discovered a thin spot up on the top side. All we can tell so far is that the wall thickness falls off there. . . ."

"All right. Keep after it, Bill."

This was more like it. If Brigadier General Straut could have this thing wapped up by the time Washington awoke to the fact that it was something big—well, he'd been waiting a long time for that second star. This was his chance, and he would damn well make the most of it.

He looked across the field at the thing. It was half in and half out of the woods, flat-sided, round-ended, featureless. Maybe he should go over and give it a closer look personally. He might spot something the others were missing. It might blow them all to kingdom come any second; but what the hell, he had earned his star on sheer guts in Normandy. He still had 'em.

He keyed the phone. "I'm coming down, Bill," he told the Major. On impulse, he strapped a pistol belt on. Not much use against a house-sized bomb, but the heft of it felt good.

The thing looked bigger than ever as the jeep approached it, bumping across the muck of the freshly plowed field. From here he could see a faint line running around, just below the juncture of side and top. Major Greer hadn't mentioned that. The line was quite obvious; in fact, it was more of a crack.

With a sound like a baseball smacking the catcher's glove, the crack opened, the upper half tilted, men sliding—then impossibly it stood open, vibrating, like the roof of a house suddenly lifted. The driver gunned the jeep. There were cries, and a ragged shrilling that set Straut's teeth on edge. The men were running back now, two of them dragging a third.

Major Greer emerged from behind the object, looked about, ran toward General Straut shouting. ". . . a man dead. It snapped; we weren't expecting it. . . ."

Straut jumped out beside the men, who had stopped now and were looking back. The underside of the gaping lid was an iridescent black. The shrill noise sounded thinly across the field. Greer arrived, panting.

"What happened?" Straut snapped.

"I was . . . checking over that thin spot, General. The first thing I knew it was . . . coming up under me. I fell; Tate was at the other side. He held on and it snapped him loose, against a tree. His skull—"

"What the devil's that racket?"

"That's the sound we were getting from inside before, General. There's something in there, alive—"

"All right, pull yourself together, Major. We're not unprepared. Bring your half-tracks into position. The tanks will be here soon."

11

Straut glanced at the men standing about. He would show them what leadership meant.

"You men keep back," he said. He puffed his cigar calmly as he walked toward the looming object. The noise stopped suddenly; that was a relief. There was a faint and curious odor in the air, something like chlorine . . . or seaweed . . . or iodine.

There were no marks in the ground surrounding the thing. It had apparently dropped straight in to its present position. It was heavy, too—the soft soil was displaced in a mound a foot high all along the side.

Behind him, Straut heard a yell. He whirled. The men were pointing; the jeep started up, churned toward him, wheels spinning. He looked up. Over the edge of the gray wall, six feet above his head, a great reddish limb, like the claw of a crab, moved, groping.

Straut yanked the .45 from its holster, jacked the action and fired. Soft matter spattered, and the claw jerked back. The screeching started up again angrily, then was drowned in the engine roar as the jeep slid to a stop.

Straut stooped, grabbed up a leaf to which a quivering lump adheared, jumped into the vehicle as it leaped forward; then a shock and they were going into a spin and . . .

"Lucky it was soft ground," somebody said. And somebody else asked, "What about the driver?"

Silence. Straut opened his eyes. "What . . . about . . ."

A stranger was looking down at him, an ordinary-looking fellow of about thirty-five.

"Easy, now, General Straut. You've had a bad spill. Everything is all right. I'm Professor Lieberman, from the University."

"The driver," Straut said with an effort.

"He was killed when the jeep went over."

"Went . . . over?"

"The creature lashed out with a member resembling a scorpion's stinger. It struck the jeep and flipped it. You were thrown clear. The driver jumped and the jeep rolled on him."

Straut pushed himself up.

"Where's Greer?"

"I'm right here, sir." Major Greer stepped up, stood attentively.

"Those tanks here yet?"

"No, sir. I had a call from General Margrave; there's some sort of holdup. Something about not destroying scientific material. I did get the mortars over from the base."

Straut got to his feet. The stranger took his arm. "You ought to lie down, General—"

"Who the hell is going to make me? Greer, get those mortars in place, spaced between your tracks."

The telephone rang. Straut seized it. "General Straut."

"General Margrave here, Straut. I'm glad you're back on your feet. There'll be some scientists from the State University coming over. Cooperate with them. You're going to have to hold things together at least until I can get another man in there to—"

"Another man? General Margrave, I'm not incapacitated. The situation is under complete control—"

13

"It is, is it? I understand you've got still another casualty. What's happened to your defensive capabilities?"

"That was an accident, sir. The jecp—"

"We'll review that matter at a later date. What I'm calling about is more important right now. The code men have made some headway on that box of yours. It's putting out a sort of transmission."

"What kind, sir?"

"Half the message—it's only twenty seconds long, repeated—is in English. It's a fragment of a recording from a daytime radio program; one of the network men here identified it. The rest is gibberish. They're still working over it."

"What—"

"Bryant tells me he thinks there may be some sort of correspondence between the two parts of the message. I wouldn't know, myself. In my opinion, it's a threat of some sort."

"I agree, General. An ultimatum."

"Right. Keep your men back at a safe distance from now on. I want no more casualties."

Straut cursed his luck as he hung up the phone. Margrave was ready to relieve him, after he had exercised every precaution. He had to do something fast, before this opportunity for promotion slipped out of his hands.

He looked at Major Greer. "I'm neutralizing this thing once and for all. There'll be no more men killed."

Lieberman stood up. "General! I must protest any attack against this—"

Straut whirled. "I'm handling this, Professor. I don't know

14

who let you in here or why—but I'll make the decisions. I'm stopping this man-killer before it comes out of its nest, maybe gets into that village beyond the woods. There are four thousand civilians there. It's my job to protect them." He jerked his head at Greer, strode out of the room.

Lieberman followed, pleading. "The creature has shown no signs of aggressiveness, General Straut—"

"With two men dead?"

"You should have kept them back—"

"Oh, it was my fault, was it?" Straut stared at Lieberman with cold fury. This civilian pushed his way in here, then had the infernal gall to accuse him, Brigadier General Straut, of causing the death of his own men. If he had the fellow in uniform for five minutes . . .

"You're not well, General. That fall—"

"Keep out of my way, Professor," Straut said. He turned and went on down the stairs. The present foul-up could ruin his career; and now this egghead interference . . .

With Greer at his side, Straut moved out to the edge of the field.

"All right, Major. Open up with your .50 calibers."

Greer called a command and a staccato rattle started up. The smell of cordite and the blue haze of gunsmoke—this was more like it. He was in command here.

Lieberman came up to Straut. "General, I appeal to you in the name of science. Hold off a little longer, at least until we learn what the message is about."

"Get back from the firing line, Professor." Straut turned his back on the civilian, raised the glasses to observe the effect of

15

the recoilless rifle. There was a tremendous smack of displaced air, and a thunderous boom as the explosive shell struck. Straut saw the gray shape jump, the raised lid waver. Dust rose from about it. There was no other effect.

"Keep firing, Greer," Straut snapped, almost with a feeling of triumph. The thing was impervious to artillery; now who was going to say it was no threat?

"How about the mortars, sir?" Greer said. "We can drop a few rounds right inside it."

"All right, try that before the lid drops."

And what we'll try next, I don't know, he thought.

The mortar fired with a muffled thud. Straut watched tensely. Five seconds later, the object erupted in a gout of pale pink debris. The lid rocked, pinkish fluid running down its opalescent surface. A second burst, and a third. A great fragment of the menacing claw hung from the branch of a tree a hundred feet from the ship.

Straut grabbed up the phone. "Cease fire!"

Lieberman stared in horror at the carnage.

The telephone rang. Straut picked it up.

"General Straut," he said, His voice was firm. He had put an end to the threat.

"Straut, we've broken the message," General Margrave said excitedly. "It's the damnedest thing I ever . . ."

Straut wanted to interrupt, announce his victory, but Margrave was droning on.

". . . strange sort of reasoning, but there was a certain analogy. In any event, I'm assured the translation is accurate. Here's how it reads in English. . . ."

16

Straut listened. Then he carefully placed the receiver back on the hook.

Lieberman stared at him.

"What did it say?"

Straut cleared his throat. He turned and looked at Lieberman for a long moment before answering.

"It said, 'Please take good care of my little girl.' "

Piers Anthony

In the Jaws
of Danger

Here is Dr. Dillingham's greatest achievement.
A whale of a tale, but a miner adventure.

The Enen—for Dr. Dillingham preferred the acronym to "North
Nebula humanoid species"—rushed in and chewed out a message-stick with machinelike dispatch. He handed it to Dillingham and stood by anxiously.

The dentist popped it into the hopper of the transcoder.
"Emergency," the little speaker said. "Only you can handle
this, Doctor!"

"You'll have to be more specific, Holmes," he said and
watched the transcoder type this onto another stick. Since the
Enens had no spoken language and he had not learned to
decipher their tooth-dents, the transcoder was the vital link in
communication.

The names he applied to the Enens were facetious. These galactics had no names in their own language, and they comprehended his humor in this regard no more than had his patients back on distant Earth. But at least they were industrious folk and very clever at physical science.

The Enen read the stick and put it between his teeth for a hurried footnote. It was amazing, Dillingham thought, how effectively they could flex their jaws for minute variations in depth and slant. Compared to this, the human jaw was a clumsy portcullis.

The message went back to the machine. "It's a big toothache that no one can cure. You must come."

"Oh, come now, Watson," Dillingham said, deeply flattered. "I've been training your dentists for six months now, and I must admit they're experienced and intelligent specialists. They know their maxillaries from their mandibulars. As a matter of fact, some of them are a good deal more adept than I, except in the specific area of metallic restorations. Surely—"

But the Enen grabbed the stick before any more could be imprinted by the machine's clattering jaws. "Doctor—this is an *alien*. It's the son of the high muckamuck of Gleep." The terms, of course, were the ones he had programmed to indicate any ruling dignitary of any other planet. He wondered whether he would be well advised to substitute more serious designations before someone caught on. Tomorrow, perhaps, he would see about it. "You, Doctor, are our only practicing exodontist."

Ah—now it was becoming clear. He was a stranger from a

far planet—and a dentist. Ergo, he must know all about off-world dentition. The Enen's faith was touching. Well, if this was a job they could not handle, he could at least take a look at it. The "alien" could hardly have stranger dentition than the Enens themselves, and success might represent a handsome credit toward his eventual freedom. It would certainly be more challenging than drilling his afternoon class in Applications of Supercolloid.

"I'm pretty busy with that new group of trainees," he said. This was merely a dodge to elicit more information, since the Enens tended to omit important details. They did not do so intentionally; it was just that their notions of importance differed here and there from his own.

"The muckamuck has offered fifty pounds of frumpstiggle for this one service," the Enen replied.

Dillingham whistled, and the transcoder dutifully printed the translation. Frumpstiggle was neither money nor merchandise. He had never been able to pin down exactly what it *was*, but for convenience thought of it as worth its exact weight in gold: $35 per ounce, $560 per pound. The Enens did not employ money as such, but their avid barter for frumpstiggle seemed roughly equivalent. His commission on fifty pounds would amount to a handsome dividend and would bring his return to Earth that much closer.

"All right," he said. "Bring the patient in."

The Enen became agitated. "The high muckamuck's family can't leave the planet. You must go to Gleep."

He had half expected something of this sort. The Enens gallivanted from planet to planet and system to system with

20

dismaying nonchalance. Dillingham had not yet become accustomed to the several ways in which they far excelled Earth technology, or to the abrupt manner of their transactions. One of their captains (strictly speaking, they didn't have officers, but this was a minor matter) had required dental help and simply stopped off at the nearest inhabited planet, skipping the normal formalities, and visited a local practitioner. Realizing that local technique was in some respects superior to that of the home planet, the captain had brought the practitioner along.

Thus Dillingham had found himself the property of the Enens—he who had never dreamed of anything other than conventional retirement in Florida. He was no intrepid spaceman, no seeker of fortune. He had been treated well enough, and certainly the Enens respected his abilities more than had his patients on Earth; but galactic intercourse was more unsettling than exciting for a man of his maturity.

"I'll go and pack my bag," he said.

II

Gleep turned out to be a water world. The ship splashed down beside a floating waystation, and they were transferred to a tanklike amphibious vehicle. It rolled into the ocean and paddled along somewhat below the surface.

Dillingham had read somewhere that intelligent life could not evolve in water because of the inhibiting effect of the liquid medium upon the motion of specialized appendages. Certainly the fish of Earth had never amounted to much. How could primitive swimmers hope to engage in interstellar commerce?

21

Evidently that particular theory was wrong, elsewhere in the galaxy. Still, he wondered just how the Gleeps had circumvented the rapid-motion barrier. Did they live in domes *under* the ocean?

He hoped the patient would not prove to be too alien. Presumably it had teeth; but that might very well be the least of the problems. At any rate, he could draw on whatever knowledge the Enens had, and he had also made sure to bring a second transcoder keyed to Gleep. It was awkward to carry two machines, but too much could be lost in retranslation if he had to get the Gleep complaints relayed through the Enens.

A monstrous whale shape loomed in the porthole. The thing spied the sub, advanced, and opened a cavernous maw. "Look out!" he yelled, wishing the driver had ears.

The Enen glanced indifferently at the message-stick and chomped a casual reply. "Everything is in order, Doctor."

"But a leviathan is about to engulf us!"

"Naturally. That's a Gleep."

Dillingham stared out the port, stunned. No wonder the citizens couldn't leave the planet! It was a matter of physics, not convention.

The vessel was already inside the colossal mouth, and the jaws were closing. "You mean—you mean this is the *patient*?" But he already had his answer. Damn those little details the Enens forgot to mention. A whale!

The mouth was shut now, and the headlight of the sub speared out to reveal encompassing mountains of flexing flesh. The treads touched land—probably the tongue—and took hold. A minute's climb brought them into a great domed air chamber.

They came to a halt beside what reminded him of the White Cliffs of Dover. The hatch sprang open, and the Enens piled out. None of them seemed concerned about the possibility that the creature might involuntarily swallow, so Dillingham put that thought as far from his mind as he was able. His skull seemed determined to hold it in, unfortunately.

"This is the tooth," the Enen's message said. The driver pointed to a solid marble boulder.

Dillingham contemplated it. The tooth stood about twelve feet high, counting only the distance it projected from the spongy gingival tissue. Much more would be below, of course.

"I see," he said. He could think of nothing more pertinent at the moment. He looked at the bag in his hand, which contained an assortment of needle-pointed probes, several ounces of instant amalgam, and sundry additional staples. In the sub was a portable drill with a heavy-duty needle attachment that could easily excavate a cavity a full inch deep.

Well, they *had* called it a "big toothache." He just hadn't been alert.

They brought forth a light extendible ladder and leaned it against the tooth. They set his drill and transcoders beside it. "Summon us when you're finished," their parting message said.

Dillingham felt automatically for the electronic signal in his pocket. By the time he drew breath to protest, the amphibian was gone.

He was alone in the mouth of a monster.

Well, he'd been in awkward situations before. He tried once

23

again to close his mind to the horrors that lurked about him and ascended the ladder, holding his lantern aloft.

The occlusive surface was about ten feet in diameter. It was slightly concave and worn smooth. In the center was a dark trench about two feet wide and over a yard long. This was obviously the source of the irritation.

He walked over to it and looked down. A putrid stench sent him gasping back. Yes—this was the cavity. It seemed to range from a foot in depth at the edges to four feet in the center. '

"That," he said aloud, "is a case of dental caries for the record book."

Unfortunately, he had no record book. All he possessed was a useless bag of implements and a smarting nose. But there was nothing for it but to explore the magnitude of the decay. It probably extended laterally within the pulp, so that the total infected area was considerably larger than that visible from above. He would have to check this directly.

He forced himself to breathe regularly, though his stomach danced in protest. He stepped down into the cavity.

The muck was ankle deep and the miasma overpowering. He summoned the dregs of his willpower and squatted to poke into the bottom with one finger. Under the slime, the surface was like packed earth. He was probably still inches from the material of the tooth itself; these were merely layers of crushed and spoiling food.

He remembered long-ago jokes about eating apple compote, pronouncing the word with an internal "s." Compost. It was not a joke anymore.

He located a dry area and scuffed it with one foot. Some

dark flakes turned up, but no real impression had been made. He wound up and drove his toe into the wall as hard as he could.

There was a thunderous roar. He clapped his hands to his ears as the air pressure increased explosively. His footing slipped, and he fell into the reeking center section of the trench.

An avalanche of muck descended upon him. Overhead, hundreds of tons of flesh and bone and gristle crashed down imperiously, seeming ready to crush every particle of matter within its compass into further compost.

The jaws were closing.

Dillingham found himself facedown in sickening garbage, his ears ringing from the atmospheric compression and his body quivering from the mechanical one. The lantern, miraculously, was undamaged and bright, and his own limbs were sound. He sat up, wiped some of the sludge from face and arms, and grabbed for the slippery light.

He was trapped between clenched jaws—inside the cavity.

Frantically he activated the signal. After an interminable period while he waited in mortal fear of suffocation, the ponderous upper jaw lifted. He scrambled out, dripping.

The bag of implements was now a thin layer of color on the surface of the tooth. "Perfect occlusion," he murmured professionally, while shaking in violent reaction to the realization that his fall had narrowly saved him from the same fate.

The ladder was gone. Anxious to remove himself from the dangerous biting surface as quickly as possible, he prepared to jump but saw a gigantic mass of tentacles reaching for his portable drill near the base of the tooth. Each tentacle appeared to be thirty feet or more in length and as strong as a python's tail.

The biting surface no longer seemed so dangerous. Dillingham remained where he was and watched the drill being carried into the darkness of the mouth's center.

In a few more minutes the amphibian vehicle appeared. The Enen driver emerged, chewed a stick, presented it. Dillingham reached for the transcoder and discovered that it was the wrong one. All he had now was the useless Gleep interpreter.

Chagrined, he fiddled with it. At least he could set it to play back whatever the Gleep prince might have said. Perhaps there had been meaning in that roar. . . .

There had been. "OUCH!" the machine exclaimed.

III

The next few hours were complicated. Dillingham now had to speak to the Enens via the Gleep muckamuck (after the episode in the cavity, he regretted this nomenclature acutely), who had been summoned for a diagnostic conference. This was accomplished by setting up shop in the creature's communications department.

The compartment was actually an offshoot from the Gleep lung, deep inside the body. It was a huge, internal air space with sensitive tentacles bunching from the walls. This was the manner in which the dominant species of this landless planet had developed fast-moving appendages whose manipulation led eventually to tools and intelligence. An entire technology had developed—*inside* the great bodies.

"So you see," he said, "I have to have an anesthetic that

will do the job, and canned air to breathe while I'm working, and a power drill that will handle up to an eighteen-inch depth of rock. Also a sledgehammer and a dozen wedges. And a derrick and the following quantities of—" He went on to make a startling list of supplies.

The transcoder sprouted half a dozen tentacles and waved them in a dizzying semaphore. After a moment a group of the wall tentacles waved back. "It shall be accomplished," the muckamuck reply came.

Dillingham wondered what visual signal had projected the "ouch!" back in the patient's mouth. Then it came to him: the tentacles that had absconded with his drill and other transcoder were extensions of the creature's tongue! Naturally they talked.

"One other thing: while you're procuring my equipment, I'd like to see a diagram of the internal structure of your molars."

"Structure?" The tentacles were agitated.

"The pattern of enamel, dentin, and pulp, or whatever passes for it in your system. A schematic drawing would do nicely. Or a sagittal section showing both the nerves and the bony socket. That tooth is still quite sensitive, which means the nerve is still alive. I wouldn't want to damage it unnecessarily."

"We have no diagrams."

Dillingham was shocked. "Don't you *know* the anatomy of your teeth? How have you repaired them before?"

"We have never had trouble with them before. We have no dentists. That is why we summoned you."

He paced the floor of the chamber, amazed. How was it

possible for such intelligent and powerful creatures to remain so ignorant of matters vital to their well-being? Never had trouble before? That cavity had obviously been festering for many years.

Yet he had faced similar ignorance daily during his Earth practice. "I'll be working blind, in that case," he said at last. "You must understand that while I'll naturally do my best, I cannot guarantee to save the tooth."

"We understand," the Gleep muckamuck replied contritely.

Back on the tooth (after a stern warning to Junior to keep those jaws apart no matter how uncomfortable things got), equipped with a face mask, respirator, elbow-length gloves, and hip boots, Dillingham began the hardest labor of his life. It was not intellectually demanding or particularly intricate— just hard. He was vaporizing the festering walls of the cavity with a thirty-pound laser drill, and in half an hour his arms were dead tired.

There *was* lateral extension of the infection. He had to wedge himself into a rotting, diminishing cavern, wielding the beam at arm's length before him. He had to twist the generator sidewise to penetrate every branching side pocket, all the while frankly terrified lest the beam slip and accidently touch part of his own body. He was playing with fire—a fiery beam that could slice off his arm and puff it into vapor in less than a careless second.

At least, he thought sweatily, he wasn't going to have to use the sledgehammer here. When he ordered the drill, he had expected a mechanical one similar to those pistons used to break up pavement on Earth. To the Gleep, however, a drill was a laser beam. This was indeed far superior to what he had had in mind. Deadly, yes—but real serendipity.

Backbreaking hours later it was done. Sterile walls of dentin lined the cavity on every side. Yet this was only the beginning.

Dillingham, after a short nap right there in the now aseptic cavity, roused himself to make careful measurements. He had to be certain that every alley was widest at the opening and that none were too sharply twisted. Wherever the measurements were unsatisfactory, he drilled away healthy material until the desired configuration had been achieved. He also adjusted the beam for "polish" and wiped away the rough surfaces.

He signalled the Enen sub and indicated by gestures that it was time for the tank of supercolloid. And resolved that *next* time he went anywhere, he would bring a trunkful of spare transcoders. He had problems enough without translation difficulties. At least he had been able to make clear that they had to send a scout back to the home planet to pick up the bulk supplies.

Supercolloid was a substance developed by the ingenious Enens in response to his exorbitant specifications of several months before. He had once entertained the notion that if he were slightly unreasonable, they would ship him home. Instead they had met the specifications exactly and increased his assessed value, neatly adding years to his term of captivity. He became more careful after that—but the substance remained a prosthodontist's dream.

Supercolloid was a fluid, stored under pressure, that set rapidly when released. It held its shape indefinitely without measurable distortion, yet was as flexible as rubber. It was ideal for difficult impressions, since it could give way while being withdrawn and spring immediately back to the proper shape. This saved time and reduced error. At 1300° Fahrenheit it melted suddenly into the thin, transparent fluid from which it started. This was its most important property.

Dillingham was about to make a very large cast. To begin the complex procedure, he had to fill every crevice of the cavity with colloid. Since the volume of the cleaned cavity came to about forty cubic feet, and supercolloid weighed fifty pounds per cubic foot when set, he required a good two thousand pounds of it, at the very least.

A full ton—to fill a single cavity. "Think big," he told himself.

He set up the tank and hauled the long hose into the pit. Once more he crawled headfirst into the lateral expansion, no longer needing the face mask. He aimed the nozzle without fear and squirted the foamy green liquid into the farthest offshoot, making certain that no air spaces remained. He backed off a few feet and filled the other crevices, but left the main section open.

In half an hour the lateral branch had been simplified considerably. It was now a deep, flat crack without offshoots. Dillingham put away the nozzle and crawled in with selected knives and brushes. He cut away projecting colloid, leaving each filling flush with the main crevice wall, and painted purple fixative over each surface.

Satisfied at last, he trotted out the colloid hose again and started the pump. This time he opened the nozzle to full aperture and filled the main crevice, backing away as the foam threatened to engulf him. Soon all of the space was full. He smoothed the green wall facing the main cavity and painted it in the same manner as the offshoots.

Now he was ready for the big one. So far he had used up about eight cubic feet of colloid, but the gaping center pit would require over thirty feet. He removed the nozzle entirely and let the tank heave itself out. The cavity was rapidly being filled.

"Turn it off," he yelled to the Enen by the pump as green foam bulged gently over the rim. One ton of supercolloid filled the tooth, and he was ready to carve it down and insert the special plastic loop in the center.

The foam continued to pump. "I said TURN IT OFF!" he cried again. Then he remembered that he had no transcoder for Enen. They could neither hear him nor comprehend him.

He flipped the hose away from the filling and aimed it over the edge of the tooth. He had no way to cut it off himself, since he had removed the nozzle. There couldn't be much left in the tank.

A rivulet of green coursed over the pink tissues, traveling toward the squidlike tongue. The tentacles reached out, grasping the foam as it solidified. They soon became festooned in green.

Dillingham laughed—but not for long. There was a steamwhistle sigh followed by a violent tremor of the entire jaw.

"I'm going to . . . sneeze," the Gleep transcoder said, sounding fuzzy.

The colloid was interfering with the articulation of the Gleep's tongue.

A sneeze! Suddenly he realized what that would mean to him and the Enen crew.

"Get under cover!" he shouted to the Enens, again forgetting that they couldn't perceive the warning. But they had already grasped the significance of the tremors and were piling into the sub frantically.

"Hey—wait for me!" But he was too late. The air howled by with the titanic intake of breath. There was a terrible pause.

Dillingham lunged for the mound of colloid and dug his fingers into the almost-solid substance. "Keep your jaws apart!" he yelled at the Gleep, praying it could still pick up the message. "KEEP THEM OPEN!"

The sound of a tornado raged out of its throat. He buried his face in green as the hurricane struck, wrenching mercilessly at his body. His arms were wrenched cruelly; his fingers tore through the infirm colloid, slipping. . . .

IV

The wind died, leaving him gasping at the edge of the tooth. He had survived it. The jaws had not closed.

He looked up. The upper cuspids hung only ten feet above, visible in the light from the charmed lamp hooked somehow to his foot.

He was past the point of reaction. "Open, please," he called in his best operative manner, hoping the transcoder was still in the vicinity, and went to peer over the edge.

32

There was no sign of the sub. The tank, with its discharging hose, was also gone.

He took a walk across the neighboring teeth, looking for whatever there was to see. He was appalled at the amount of decalcification and outright decay in evidence. This Gleep child would shortly be in pain again, unless substantial restorative work was done immediately.

But in a shallow cavity—one barely a foot deep—he found the transcoder. "It's an ill decalcification that bodes nobody good," he murmured, retrieving it.

The sub reappeared and disgorged its somewhat shaken passengers. Dillingham marched back over the rutted highway and joined them. But the question still nagged his mind: how could the caries he had observed be reconciled with the muckamuck's undoubtedly sincere statement that there had never been dental trouble before? What had changed?

He carved the green surface into an appropriate pattern and carefully applied his fixative. He was ready for the next step.

Now the derrick was brought up and put in play. Dillingham guided its dangling hook into the eyelet set in the colloid and signaled the Enen operator to lift. The chain went taut; the mass of solidified foam eased grandly out of its socket and hung in the air, an oddly shaped boulder.

He turned his attention to the big crevice filling. He screwed in a corkscrew eyelet and arranged a pulley so that the derrick could act on it effectively. The purple fixative had prevented the surface of the main impression from attaching to that of the subsidiary one—just as it was also protecting the several smaller branches within.

There was no real trouble. In due course every segment of

the impression was marked and laid out in the makeshift laboratory he had set up near the waterlift of the Gleep's mouth. They were ready for one more step.

The tank of prepared investment arrived. This, too, was a special composition. It remained fluid until triggered by a particular electric jolt, whereupon it solidified instantly. Once solid, it could not be affected by anything short of demolition by a sledgehammer.

Dillingham pumped a quantity into a great temporary vat. He attached a plastic handle to the smallest impression, dipped it into the vat, withdrew it entirely covered by white batter and touched the electrode to it. He handed the abruptly solid object to the nearest Enen.

Restorative procedure on Gleep differed somewhat from established Earth technique. All it took was a little human imagination and Enen technology.

The octopus-tongue approached while he worked. It reached for him. "Get out of here or I'll cram you into the burnout furnace!" he snapped into the transcoder. The tongue retreated.

The major section was a problem. It barely fit into the vat, and a solid foot of it projected over the top. He finally had the derrick lower it until it bumped bottom, then raise it a few inches and hold it steady. He passed out brushes, and he and the Enen crew went to work slopping the goo over the top and around the suspending hook.

He touched the electrode to the white monster. The derrick lifted the mass, letting the empty vat fall free. Yet another stage was done.

Two ovens were employed for the burnout. Each was big enough for a man to stand in. They placed the ends of the plastic rods in special holders and managed to fit all of the smaller units into one oven, fastening them into place by means of a heat-resistant framework. The main chunk sat in the other oven, propped upside-down.

They sealed the ovens and set their thermostats for 2000°. Dillingham lay down in the empty vat and slept.

Three hours later burnout was over. Even supercolloid took time to melt completely when heated in a fifteen-hundred-pound mass. But now the green liquid had been drained into reservoirs and sealed away, while the smaller quantities of melted plastic were allowed to collect in a disposal vat. The white investments were hollow shells, open only where the plastic rods had projected.

The casting was the most spectacular stage. Dillingham had decided to use gold, though he worried that its high specific gravity would overbalance the Gleep jaw. It was impossible under present conditions to arrange for a gold-plated, matching-density filling, and he was not familiar enough with other metals to be sure they were adaptable to his purpose. The expansion coefficient of his investment matched that of gold exactly, for example; anything else would solidify into the wrong size.

Gold, at any rate, was nothing to the muckamuck; his people refined it through their gills, extracting it from the surrounding water on order in any quantity.

The crucible arrived: a self-propelled boilerlike affair. They piled hundred-pound ingots of precise gold alloy into the hopper, while the volcanic innards of the crucible rumbled and belched and melted everything to rich bright liquid.

A line of Enens carried the smaller investments, which were shaped inside exactly like the original impressions, to the spigot and held them with tongs while the fluid fortune poured in. These were carefully deposited in the vat, now filled with cold water.

The last cast, of course, was the colossal vat-shaped one. This was simply propped up under the spigot while the tired crew kept feeding in ingots.

By the time this cast had been poured, twenty-four tons of gold had been used in all.

While the largest chunk was being hauled to the ocean inside the front of the mouth, Dillingham broke open the smaller investments and laid out the casts according to his chart of the cavity. He gave each a minimum of finishing; on so gross a scale, it could hardly make much difference.

The finished casts weighed more than twenty times as much as the original colloid impressions had, and even the smallest ones were distinctly awkward to maneuver into place. He marked them, checked off their positions on his chart, and had the Enens ferry them up with the derrick. At the other end, he manhandled each into its proper place, verified its fit and position and withdrew it to paint it with cement. No part of this filling would come loose in action.

Once again the branching cavern lost its projections, this time permanently, as each segment was secured and severed from its projecting sprue. He kept the sprues—the handles of gold, the shape of the original plastic handles—on until the end, because otherwise there would have been no purchase on the weighty casts. He had to have some handle to adjust them.

The derrick lowered the crevice-piece into the cavity. Two Enens pried it in with power crowbars. Dillingham stood by and squirted cement over the mass as it slid reluctantly into the hole.

It was necessary to attach a heavy weight to the derrick-hook and swing it repeatedly against the four-ton cast in order to tamp it in all the way.

At last it was time for the major assembly. Nineteen tons of gold descended slowly into the hole while they dumped quarts of liquid cement into a pool below. The cast touched bottom and settled into place, while the cement bubbled up around the edges and overflowed.

They danced a little jig on top of the filling—just to tamp it in properly, Dillingham told himself, wishing that a fraction of its value in Earth terms could be credited to his purchase-price. The job was over.

V

"A commendable performance," the high muckamuck said. "My son is frisking about in his pen like a regular tadpole and eating well."

Dillingham remembered what he had seen during the walk along the occlusive surfaces. "I'm afraid he won't be frisking long. In another year or two he'll be feeling half a dozen other caries. Decay is rampant."

"You mean this will happen again?" The tentacles waved so violently that the transcoder stuttered.

Dillingham decided to take the fish by the tail. "Are you still trying to tell me that no member of your species has suffered dental caries before this time?"

"Never."

This still did not make sense. "Does your son's diet differ in any important respect from yours, or from that of other children?"

"My son is a prince!"

"Meaning he can eat whatever he wants, whether it is good for him or not?"

The Gleep paused. "He gets so upset if he doesn't have his way. He's only a baby—hardly three centuries old."

Dillingham was getting used to differing standards. "Do you feed him delicacies—refined foods?"

"Naturally. Nothing but the best."

He sighed. "Muckamuck, my people also had perfect teeth—until they began consuming sweets and overly refined foods. Then dental caries became the most common disease among them. You're going to have to curb your boy's appetite."

"I couldn't." He could almost read the agitation of the tentacles without benefit of translation. "He'd throw a terrible tantrum."

He had expected this reaction. He'd encountered it many times on Earth. "In that case, you'd better begin training a crew of dentists. Your son will require constant attention."

"But we can't do such work ourselves. We have no suitable appendages, externally."

"Import some dentists, then. You have no alternative."

The creature signaled a sigh. "You make a convincing case." The tentacles relaxed while it thought. Suddenly they came alive again. "Enen—it seems we need a permanent technician. Will you sell us this one?"

Dillingham gaped, horrified at the thought of all that garbage in the patient's jaw. Surely they couldn't—

"Sell him!" the Enen chief replied angrily. Dillingham wondered how he was able to understand the words, then realized that his transcoder was picking up the Gleep signals translated by the other machine. From the Enen to Gleep to English, via paired machines. Why hadn't he thought of that before?

"This is a human being," the Enen continued indignantly. "A member of an intelligent species dwelling far across the galaxy. He is the only exodontist in this entire sector of space, and a fine upstanding fellow at that. How dare you make such a crass suggestion!"

Bless him! Dillingham had always suspected that his hosts were basically creatures of principle.

"We're prepared to offer a full ton of superlative-grade frumpstiggle . . ." the muckamuck said enticingly.

"A full *ton?*" The Enens were aghast. Then, recovering: "True, the Earthman *has* taught us practically all he knows. We could probably get along without him now. . . ."

"Now wait a minute!" Dillingham shouted; but the bargaining continued unabated.

After all—what is the value of a man, compared to frumpstiggle?

Eric Frank Russell

The Witness

*It was a trial by fury, with the alien facing
trumped-up charges. But the Council for
Defense held two unbeatable cards.*

No court in history had drawn so much world attention. Six
television cameras swivelled slowly as they followed red and
black robed legal lights parading solemnly to their seats. Ten
microphones sent the creaking of shoes and rustling of papers
over national networks in both hemispheres. Two hundred
reporters and special correspondents filled a gallery reserved
for them alone. Forty representatives of cultural organizations
stared across the court at twice their number of governmental
and diplomatic officials sitting blank-faced and impassive.

Tradition had gone by the board; procedure resembled nothing familiar to the average lawyer, for this was a special
occasion devised to suit a special case. Technique had
been adapted to cope with a new and extraordinary cul-
prit, while the dignity of justice was upheld by means of stagy
trimmings.

There were five judges and no jury, but a billion citizens were in their homes watching and listening, determined to ensure fair play. Ideas of what constituted fair play were as varied as the unseen audience, and most of them unreasoning, purely emotional. A minority of spectators hoped for life, many lusted for death, while the waverers compromised in favor of arbitrary expulsion, each according to how he had been in-fluenced by the vast flood of colorful and bigoted propaganda preceding this event.

The judges took their places with the casual unconcern of those too old and deeply sunk in wisdom to notice the lime-light. A hush fell, broken only by the ticking of the large clock over their rostrum. It was the hour of ten in the morning of May 17, 1977. The microphones sent the ticking around the world. The cameras showed the judges, the clock, and finally settled on the center of all this attention: the creature in the defendant's box.

Six months ago this latter object had been the sensation of the century, the focal point of a few wild hopes and many wilder fears. Since then it had appeared so often on the video screens, magazine and newspaper pages, that the public sense of amazement had departed, while the hopes and fears re-mained. It had slowly degenerated to a cartoon character con-temptuously dubbed "Spike," depicted as halfway between a hopelessly malformed imbecile and the crafty emissary of a craftier otherworld enemy. Familiarity had bred contempt, but not enough of it to kill the fears.

Its name was Maeth and it came from some planet in the region of Procyon. Three feet high, bright green, with feet

41

that were mere pads, and stubby limbs fitted with suckers and cilia, it was covered in spiky protrusions and looked somewhat like an educated cactus. Except for its eyes, great golden eyes that looked upon men in naive expectation of mercy, because it had never done anyone any harm. A toad, a wistful toad, with jewels in its head.

Pompously, a black gowned official announced, "This special court, held by international agreement, and convened within the area of jurisdiction of the Federal Government of the United States of America, is now in session! Silence!"

The middle judge glanced at his fellows, adjusted his spectacles, peered gravely at the toad, or cactus, or whatever it might be. "Maeth of Procyon, we are given to understand that you can neither hear nor speak, but you can comprehend us telepathically and respond visually."

Cameras focussed as Maeth turned to the blackboard immediately behind him and chalked one word. "Yes."

"You are accused," the judge went on, "generally of illegal entry into this world known as Earth and specifically into the United States of America. Do you plead guilty or not guilty?"

"How else can one enter?" inquired Maeth, in bold white letters.

The judge frowned. "Kindly answer my question."

"Not guilty."

"You have been provided with defending counsel—have you any objection to him?"

"Blessed be the peacemaker."

Few relished that crack. It smacked of the Devil quoting Scripture.

Making a sign, the judge leaned back, polished his glasses. Adjusting the robes on his shoulders, the prosecuting attorney came to his feet. He was tall, hatchet-faced, sharp-eyed.

"First witness!"

A thin, reedy man came out of the well of the court, took his chair, sat uncomfortably, with fidgeting hands.

"Name?"

"Samuel Nall."

"You farm outside Dansville?"

"Yes, sir. I—"

"Do not call me 'sir.' Just reply to my questions. It was upon your farm that this creature made its landing?"

"Your Honors, I object!" Mr. Defender stood up, a fat, florid man, but deceptively nimble-witted. "My client is a person, not a creature. It should therefore be referred to as the defendant."

"Objection overruled," snapped the middle judge. "Proceed, Mr. Prosecutor."

"It was upon your farm that this *creature* landed?"

"Yes," said Samuel Nall, staring pridefully at the cameras. "It come down all of a sudden and—"

"Confine yourself to the question. The arrival was accompanied by much destruction?"

"Yes."

"How much?"

"Two barns and a dollop of crops. I'm down three thousand dollars."

"Did this *creature* show any remorse?"

"None." Nall scowled across the court. "Acted like it couldn't care less."

Mr. Prosecutor seated himself, throwing a mock smile at the fat man. "Your witness."

Standing up, the latter eyed Nall benevolently and inquired, "Were these barns of yours octagonal towers with walls having moveable louvres and with barometrically-controlled roofs?"

Samuel Nall waggled his eyebrows and uttered a faint, "Huh?"

"Never mind. Dismiss that query and answer me this one: were your crops composed of foozles and bicolored merkins?"

In desperation, Nall said, "It was ripe barley."

"Dear me! Barley—how strange! Don't you know what foozles and merkins are? Wouldn't you recognize them if you saw them?"

"I reckon not," admitted Farmer Nall, with much reluctance.

"Permit me to observe that you seem singularly lacking in perceptive faculties," remarked Mr. Defender, tartly. "Indeed, I am really sorry for you. Can you detect sorrow in my face?"

"I dunno," said Nall, feeling that his throne before the cameras was becoming somehow like a bed of nails.

"In other words, you cannot recognize remorse when you see it?"

"Objection!" roared Mr. Prosecutor, coming up crimson. "The witness cannot reasonably be expected—" He stopped as his opponent sat down. Recovering swiftly, he growled, "Next witness!"

Number two was big, beefy, clad in blue, and had all the assurance of one long familiar with courts and the tedious processes of the law.

"Name?"

"Joseph Higginson."

"You are an officer of the Dansville police?"

"Correct."

"You were summoned by the first witness?"

"I was."

Mr. Prosecutor wore the smile of one in complete command of circumstances as he went on, "Discovering what had occurred, you tried to apprehend the cause of it, did you not?"

"I sure did." Officer Higginson turned his head, threw a scowl at the golden eyes pleading in the box.

"And what happened?"

"It paralyzed me with a look."

The judge on the left interjected, "You appear to have recovered. How extensive was this paralysis, and how long did it last?"

"It was complete, Your Honor, but it wore off after a couple of hours."

"By which time," said Mr. Prosecutor, taking over again, "this outlandish object had made good its escape?"

Lugubriously, "Yes."

"It therefore obstructed a police officer in the execution of his duty, assaulted a police officer, and resisted arrest?"

"It did," agreed Higginson, with emphasis.

"Your witness." Mr. Prosecutor seated himself, well satisfied.

Mr. Defender arose, hooked thumbs in vest holes, and inquired with disarming amiability, "You can recognize another police official when you see him?"

"Naturally."

"Very well. There is one at present seated in the public section. Kindly point him out for the benefit of this court."

Higginson looked carefully over the small audience which represented in person the vaster audience beyond. Cameras swung in imitation of his search. Judges, reporters, officials, all looked the same way.

"He must be in plain clothes," declared Higginson, giving up.

The middle judge interposed mildly, "This court can hardly accept witness's inability to recognize a plain clothes officer as evidence."

"No, Your Honor," agreed Mr. Defender. His plump features registered frustration and disappointment which gladdened the heart of his watching opponent. Then, satisfied that the other had reached the heights, he plunged him to the depths by brightening and adding, "But the said official is in full uniform."

Mr. Prosecutor changed faces like swapping masks. Higginson got a crick in the neck as he took in the audience again.

"Olive-drab with red trimmings," Mr. Defender went on. "He is a Provost Marshal of the Corps of Military Police."

"You didn't tell me that," Higginson pointed out. He was openly aggrieved.

"Did you tell the defendant that you were a police officer?"

The witness reddened, opened his mouth, closed it, gazed appealingly at the prosecuting attorney.

"Answer the question!" insisted a judge.

"No, I did not tell it."

"Why not?"

Mopping his forehead, Higginson said in hoarse tones, "Didn't think it was necessary. It was obvious, wasn't it?"

"It is for me to put the questions; for you to provide the answers. Do you agree that the Provost Marshal is obvious?"

"Objection!" Mr. Prosecutor waved for attention. "Opinions are not evidence."

"Sustained!" responded the middle judge. He eyed the defending attorney over his glasses. "This court takes cognisance of the fact that there was no need for witness to offer vocally any information available to defendant telepathically. Proceed with your examination."

Mr. Defender returned his attention to Higginson and asked, "Precisely what were you doing at the moment you were paralyzed?"

"Aiming my gun."

"And about to fire?"

"Yes."

"At the defendant?"

"Yes."

"Is it your habit to fire first and ask questions afterward?"

"The witness's habits are not relevant," put in the middle judge. He looked at Higginson. "You may ignore that question."

Officer Higginson grinned his satisfaction and duly ignored it.

"From what range were you about to fire?" pursued the defending attorney.

"Fifty or sixty yards."

"So far? You are an excellent marksman?"

Higginson nodded, without pride, and warily. The plump man, he had decided, was a distinct pain in the neck.

"About what time do you hope to get home for supper?"

Caught on one foot by this sudden shift of attack, the witness gaped and said, "Maybe midnight."

"Your wife will be happy to know that. Were it not for the radio and video, you could not have told her vocally, could you?"

"I can't bawl from here to Dansville," assured Higginson, slightly sarcastic.

"Of course not. Such a distance is completely beyond range of the unaided human voice." Mr. Defender rubbed his chin, mused awhile, suddenly demanded, "Can you bawl *telepathically* for fifty to sixty yards?"

No reply.

"Or is your mental limit in keeping with what the defendant assures me to be the normal limit of twenty-five to thirty yards?"

Higginson screwed up his eyes and said nothing.

"Don't you know?"

"No."

"A pity!" commented Mr. Defender, shaking his head sadly and taking a seat.

* * *

The third witness was a swarthy, olive-skinned character who stared sullenly at his boots while the prosecuting attorney got to work.

"Name?"

"Dominic Lolordo." He gave it an undertone, as if reluctant to have it coupled with his image on the video.

"You operate a seafood restaurant?"

"Yes."

"Do you recognize the creature in that box?"

His eyes slid sidewise. "Yes."

"In what circumstances did you last see it?"

"In my joint, after hours."

"It had forced an entrance, had it not, shortly before dawn, and it awakened you while plundering the place?"

"That's correct."

"You did not try to catch it?"

Lolordo made a face. "Catch that? *Look* at it!"

"Appearance alone would not deter you if you were being robbed," Mr. Prosecutor suggested meaningly. "Surely there was something else?"

"It had walked in through the window," said Lolordo, his voice rising considerably. "Right through the window, leaving a hole its own shape. It went out the same way, making another hole. No broken glass around, no splinters, nothing. What can you do with a green nightmare that walks through glass as if it wasn't there?"

"Seeing this demonstration of supernormal powers, you ran for assistance?"

"You bet!"

"But it came too late? This unscrupulous plunderer had gone?"

"Yes."

The questioner handed over with a gesture, and the defending attorney began.

"You assert you were plundered? Of what?"

"Stuff."

"That is not an answer."

"Ain't it?" Lolordo yawned with exaggerated disinterest.

The middle judge bent forward, frowning heavily. "Does the witness desire to be committed for contempt?"

"Lobsters and oysters," said Lolordo, hurriedly and with bad grace.

"In other words, a square meal?" inquired Mr. Defender.

"If that's what you want to call it."

"Was it being consumed as if the defendant were ravenously hungry?"

"I didn't stick around to see. I took one look and went on my way—fast."

"So that if the defendant picked up enough of your thoughts to realize that a felonious act had been committed, there was no opportunity to apologize or make restitution?"

No reply.

"And, in any case, your departing thoughts were violently hostile?"

"I wasn't hot-footing for a bouquet," assured Lolordo.

Mr. Defender said to the judges, "This witness is impertinent. I have no further use for him."

The judges conferred, and the middle one decided coldly,

"The witness will be detained within the precincts of this court until the case has been decided."

Lolordo stamped away from his seat, glowering right and left.

"Fourth witness!"

The chair was taken by a middle-aged, dapper man who resembled the movie notion of a bank president or an eminent surgeon. He could have been cast equally well for either part.

"Name."

"Winthrop Allain."

"You are a resident professor of zoology, are you not?" inquired the prosecuting attorney.

"That is correct."

"You recognize the creature in the box?"

"I ought to. I have been in close communication with it for many weeks."

Mr. Prosecutor made an impatient gesture. "In what circumstances did you first encounter it?"

An answer to that one seemed unnecessary. The whole world knew the circumstances, had been told them time and time again with many fanciful frills.

Nevertheless, Allain responded, "It appeared in the zoo some two hours after closing time. How it got there I don't know."

"It was snooping around, seeing all there was to see, making mental notes of everything?"

Hesitantly, "Well—"

"Was it or was it not looking over the place?"

"It certainly saw a good bit of the zoo before the keepers discovered it, but—"

"Please do not embellish your answers, Professor Allain," said Mr. Prosecutor, firmly. "Let us continue: owing to the great furor created by this strange object's arrival and subsequent exploits, your keepers had no difficulty in recognizing it?"

"None at all. They reported to me at once."

"What did you do then?"

"I attended to the matter myself. I found it a warm and comfortable apartment in the unused section of the Reptile House."

The entire court along with the cameras peered respectfully at the expert who could treat such an occasion with such nonchalance.

"How did you achieve this without suffering paralysis, disintegration, or some other unnatural fate?" Mr. Prosecutor's voice had a touch of acid. "Did you graciously extend a cordial invitation?"

The witness, dryly, "Precisely!"

"There is a time and place for humor, Professor," reproved Mr. Prosecutor, with some severity. "However, the court understands that you classified this nightmarish entity as a reptile and managed to put it in its proper place."

"Nonsense! The Reptile House was immediately available, convenient, and acceptable. The defendant is unclassifiable."

Dismissing that with a contemptuous gesture, the prosecuting attorney went on, "You are not prepared to tell this court by what means you overcame this creature's menacing powers and succeeded in trapping it?"

"I did not trap it. I knew it was sentient and treated it as such."

"If we can rely upon the evidence of other witnesses," said Mr. Prosecutor, tartly, "you were fortunate to have any choice about the matter. Why did this caricature permit you to make the contact it denied to others?"

"Because it recognized my mind as of a type accustomed to dealing with nonhuman forms. With considerable logic it assumed that contact with me would be far easier than with any others."

"With considerable logic," echoed the prosecuting attorney, turning toward the judges. "I ask Your Honors to make especial note of that remark, bearing in mind that witness has a distinguished status." He returned his attention to Allain. "By that, you mean it is intelligent?"

"Indubitably!"

"You have had many weeks in which to study the mind of this unwanted invader. Just how intelligent would you say it is?"

"As much so as we are, though in a different way."

"Do you consider this sample to be fairly representative of its race?"

"I have no reason to suppose otherwise."

"Which race, therefore, equals us in brainpower?"

"Very probably." Professor Allain rubbed his chin and mused a moment. "Yes, insofar as one can relate things which are not the same, I'd say they are our intellectual equals."

"Perhaps our superiors, not only in brains, but also in numbers?"

"I don't know. I doubt it."

"The possibility cannot be ruled out?" persisted Mr. Prosecutor.

"Such data as is available is far from sufficient and therefore I—"

"Do not evade my question. There is a possibility, no matter how remote, that the life-form represented by this monster now standing before us is the direst menace humanity has ever been called upon to face?"

"Anything can be construed as a menace if you insist, but—"

"A *menace*, yes or no?"

The middle judge interjected profoundly, "Witness cannot be required to provide a positive answer to a hypothetical question."

Not fazed in the least, Mr. Prosecutor bowed. "Very well, Your Honor, I will put it differently." He resumed with Allain. "In your expert estimation, is the intelligence quotient of this life-form high enough to enable it to conquer, subdue, and enslave humanity if it so desired?"

"I do not know."

"That is your only answer?"

"I'm afraid so."

"It is quite satisfactory," commented Mr. Prosecutor, throwing a significant look through the cameras at the unseen but billion-strong jury, "inasmuch as it admits the possibility of peril, extreme peril."

"I did not say that," protested Allain.

"Neither have you said the contrary," retorted the other. He seated himself, confident and pleased. "Your witness."

Mr. Defender began heavily, "Professor Allain, have your various handouts concerning the defendant been reported factually?"

"Without exception, they have been grossly distorted," said Allain, grimly. He cast a cold look at the big group of reporters who grinned back arrogantly.

"The defendant has repeatedly been described as a spy who must receive drastic treatment lest worse befall. Does your data support that theory?"

"No."

"What status do you assign to the defendant?"

"A refugee," said Allain.

"It is impossible for the defendant's motives to be hostile?"

"Nothing is impossible," said Professor Allain, honest though the heavens fall. "The smartest of us can be fooled. But I don't think I am fooled. That is my opinion, for what it is worth."

Mr. Defender sighed, "As I have been reminded, opinions are not evidence." He sat down murmuring, "Most unfortunate! Most unfortunate!"

"Fifth witness!"

"Tenth witness!"

"Sixteenth witness!"

That one, number sixteen, ended the prosecution's roster. Four or five times as many witnesses could have been produced, but these were the pick of the bunch. They had something cogent to offer, something calculated to help the public decide once and for all—at least with its prejudices if not with its brains—whether gallivanting life-forms were to be tolerated, or given the bum's rush, or worse. The question at issue was the ephemeral one of public safety, and it was for the public to say whether or not they were going to take any risks. With this in mind, the evidence of the sixteenth made a formidable indictment against the queer, golden-eyed thing on trial for its liberty or even its life.

Conscious that he was leading on points, Mr. Prosecutor came erect, gazed authoritatively at the defendant.

"Just why did you come to this world?"

"To escape my own."

"Do you expect us to believe that?"

"I expect nothing," chalked Maeth laboriously. "I merely hope."

"You hope for what?"

"For kindness."

It disconcerted the questioner. Left with no room for a telling retort, he was silent for a moment while he sought another angle.

"Then your own world did not please you? What was wrong with it?"

"Everything," responded Maeth.

"Meaning you were a misfit?"

"Yes."

"Nevertheless you view *this* world as a suitable dumping-ground for misfits?"

No reply.

"I suggest that your plea is nonsense, your whole story a sheer fabrication. I suggest that your motives in coming here are deeper and darker than you dare admit. I will go further and put it to you that you do not come even from the region of Procyon, but from somewhere a good deal nearer, such as Mars."

Still no reply.

"Are you aware that astronomical engineers have subjected your damaged ship to long and careful examination and made a report on it?"

Maeth stood there, pathetically patient, eyes looking into the distance as if in search of peace, and said nothing.

"Are you aware that they have reported that while your vessel is far in advance of anything yet developed by us, and while it is undoubtedly capable of traveling far outside this solar system, it is not able to reach Alpha Centauri, much less Procyon?"

"That is true," wrote Maeth on the board.

"Yet you maintain that you came from the region of Procyon?"

"Yes."

The prosecuting attorney spread despairing hands. "You have heard the defendant, Your Honors. His ship cannot reach here from Procyon. All the same, it came from Procyon. This creature cannot manage to be consistent, either because it is dimwitted or, more probably, an ineffectual liar. I therefore see little purpose in continuing my—"

"I rode on a rock," scrawled Maeth.

"There!" Mr. Prosecutor pointed sardonically at the blackboard. "The defendant rode on a rock. That is the escape from a self-created impasse—a rock, no less!" He frowned at the box. "You must have ridden a long, long way."

57

"I did."

"So you sat your ship on this rock and saved fuel by letting it carry you many millions of miles? Have you any idea of the mathematical odds against finding a wandering asteroid in any section of space?"

"They are very large," admitted Maeth.

"Yet you discovered the very asteroid to bring you all the way here? Most astonishing spacemanship, is it not?"

"It did not bring me all the way. It brought me most of the way."

"All right," agreed Mr. Prosecutor, with airy contempt. "Ninety-nine million instead of one hundred million or whatever the distance is supposed to be. It is still amazing."

"Moreover," continued Maeth, writing steadily, "I did not select one to bring me here, as you imply. I thankfully used the only visible rock to take me anywhere. I had no specific destination. I fled into the void at random, putting my trust in the fates."

"So some other rock might have borne you some place else, might it not?"

"Or no place at all," Maeth put morbidly. "The fates were kind."

"Don't be too sure of that." Mr. Prosecutor hooked thumbs in vest pockets and studied the other with sinister expression. "If your real purposes, your real motives are in fact those which have been attributed to you by our ever-alert news services, it is to be expected that you would have a cover-up story replete with plausibility. You have given this court such a story, but have offered no concrete evidence in proof. We are left with nothing but your unsupported word—and the word of an ill-

58

formed alien, an unknown quantity, at that!" He paused, ended, "Can you not submit to this court something more material than a series of bald assertations?"

"I have no way of combating disbelief," wrote Maeth, slowly and tiredly, "except with trust."

Mr. Prosecutor countered that one by striking hard and ruthlessly. "How many others of your kind are now upon this world, following their dastardly designs while you distract attention by posing in the full glare of publicity?"

The court, the hidden audience, had not thought of that. Half a dozen reporters quietly kicked themselves for not having conceived it first and played it up for all it was worth. It had been assumed from the beginning that the alien in their hands was the only one on the planet. Yet there might well be more, a dozen, a hundred, hiding in the less frequented places, skulking in the shadows, biding their time. People stared at each other and fidgeted uneasily.

"I came alone," Maeth put on the board.

"I accept that statement. It may be the only truthful one you have made. Experts report that your vessel is a single-seater scout, so obviously you came in it alone. But how many other vessels came about the same time?"

"None."

"It would be a comfort to think so," remarked Mr. Prosecutor, thereby discomforting his listeners. "Doubtless, your world has many other ships, much larger and more powerful than yours?"

"Many," admitted Maeth. "But they can go no farther or faster. They can only bear greater loads."

"How did you come by your own ship?"

"I stole it."

"Indeed?" The prosecuting attorney raised his eyebrows, gave a little laugh. "A self-confessed thief!" He assumed an air of broadminded understanding. "It is expected, of course, that one would suffer less by confessing to theft rather than espionage." He let that sink in before attempting another hard blow. "Would you care to tell us how many other bold and adventurous males are ready or making ready to follow your path of conquest?"

The defending attorney stood up and said, "I advise my client not to answer."

His opponent waved him down, turned to the judges. "Your Honors, I am ready to state my case."

They consulted the clock, talked in undertones between themselves, then said, "Proceed."

The speech for the prosecution was able, devastating and long. It reviewed the evidence, drew dark conclusions, implied many other things from which the hidden audience could draw other and still darker conclusions. This is not to say that Mr. Prosecutor had any real hatred of, or fear of, the stranger at the gate; it was merely that he was doing his specialized job with ability that was considerable.

"This case, with its own new and peculiar routine," he reminded, "will go down in legal annals. As from today it will constitute a precedent by which we shall determine our attitude toward future visitors from space. And the final arbiters of that attitude will be *you*, the members of the general public, who will reap the reward of outside alliances or"—he paused, hardened his voice—"suffer the sorrows of otherworld enmities. Allow me to emphasize that the rewards can be small, pitifully small, while the sorrows can be immense!"

Clearing his throat, he had a sip of water, started to get into his stride. "In trying to decide what should be done for the best, we have no basis for forming conclusions other than that provided by the fantastic example who will be the subject of your verdict."

Turning, he stared at Maeth while he went on. "This creature has not been put on oath because we know of no oath binding upon it. Its ethics—if any—are its own, having little in common with ours. All we do know is that its farfetched and highly imaginative story places such a strain upon human credulity that any one of us might be forgiven for deeming it a shameless liar."

Maeth's large eyes closed in pain, but Mr. Prosecutor went determinedly on. "While the question of its truthfulness, or lack of same, may remain a matter of speculation, we do have some evidence based upon fact. We know, for instance, that it has no respect for property or the law, which forms of respect are the very foundation-stones of the civilization we have built through the centuries and intend to preserve against all comers."

He overdid it there. Maeth was too small, too wide-eyed and alone to fit the part of a ruthless destroyer of civilizations. Nevertheless, the picture would serve to sway opinions. Some thousands, probably millions, would argue that when in doubt it is best to play safe.

"A thief. More than that: a self-admitted thief who steals not only from us but also from his own," declared the prosecuting attorney, quite unconscious of switching his pronoun from neuter to male. "A destroyer, and an intelligent one, possibly the forerunner of a host of destroyers. I say that advisedly, for where one can go an army can follow." Dismissing the question of whence said army was going to get its flock of transcosmic asteroids, he added, "A dozen armies!"

His voice rising and falling, hardening and softening, he played expertly upon the emotions of his listeners, as a master would play on a giant organ, appealing to world patriotism, pandering to parochialism, justifying prejudices, enlarging fears—fear of self, fear of others, fear of the strange in shape, fear of tomorrow, fear of the unknown. Solemnity, ridicule, sonorousness, sarcasm, all were weapons in his vocal armory.

"He," Mr. Prosecutor said, pointing at Maeth and still using the male pronoun, "he pleads for admission as a citizen of this world. Do we take him with all his faults and follies, with all his supernormal powers and eccentric aptitudes, with all his hidden motives that may become clear only when it is too late? Or, if indeed he be as pure and innocent as he would have us believe, would it not be better to inflict upon him a grave injustice rather than court infinitely greater injustices to a great number?"

Challengingly he stared around. "If we take him, as a refugee, who will have him? Who will accept the society of a creature with which the average human has no joint understanding?" He gave a short, sharp laugh. "Oh, yes, there have been requests for the pleasure of his company. Incredible as it may seem, there are people who want him."

Holding up a letter for all to see, he continued, "This person offers him a home. Why? Well, the writer claims that he himself was a spiky thing in Procyon during his eighth incarnation." He tossed the letter on his desk. "The crackpots are always with us. Fortunately, the course of human history will be decided by calmly reasoning citizens and not by incurable nuts."

For a further half hour he carried on, a constant flow of words which concluded with "In human affairs there is a swift end for the human spy, quick riddance for the suspected spy. I can conceive of no reason why any alien form deserves treatment more merciful than that which we accord to fellow humans. Here, we have before us one who at very least is an undesirable character, at most the first espionage agent of a formidable enemy. It is the prosecution's case that you have to consider *only* whether it is in the best interest of public safety that he be rewarded with death or with summary expulsion into the space from which he came. The weight of evidence rules out all other alternatives. You will not have failed to note that the witnesses who have appeared are overwhelmingly for the prosecution. Is it not remarkable that there is not one witness for the defense?" He waited to give it time to sink home, then drove it further by repeating, "Not one!"

Another sip of water, after which he seated himself, carefully smoothed the legs of his pants.

One thing seemed fairly clear: Maeth was a stinker.

Mr. Defender created a mild stir right at the start by rising and saying, "Your Honors, the defense does not intend to state its case."

The judges peered at him as if he were a sight ten times more strange than his own client. They pawed papers, talked together in whispers.

In due time, the middle one inquired, "By that, do you mean that you surrender to verdict by public poll?"

"Eventually, of course, Your Honor, but not just yet. I wish to produce evidence for my side and will be content to let my case rest on that."

"Proceed," ordered the judge, frowning doubtfully.

Addressing Maeth, the defending attorney said, "On your home world all are like you, namely, telepathic and nonvocal?"

"Yes, everyone."

"They share a common neural band, or, to put it more simply, they think with a communal mind?"

"Yes."

"That is the essential feature in which your home world differs from this one of ours: that its people share a racial mind, thinking common thoughts?"

"Yes," chalked Maeth.

"Tell this court about your parents."

Maeth's eyes closed a moment, as if the mind behind them had gone far, far away.

"My parents were freaks of nature. They drifted from the common band until they had almost lost contact with the race-mind."

"That was something the race-mind could not tolerate?" asked Mr. Defender gently.

"No."

"So they were killed—*for having minds of their own?*"

A long pause and a slow "Yes." The scrawl on the board was thin, shaky, barely decipherable.

"As you would have been had you not fled in sheer desperation?"

"Yes."

Mr. Defender eyed the judges. "I would like to put further questions to the fourth witness."

They signed agreement, and Professor Allain found his way back to the chair.

"Professor, as an expert who has made a long, personal study of my client, will you tell this court whether the defendant is old or young."

"Young," said Allain promptly.

"Very young?"

"Fairly young," Allain responded. "Not quite an adult."

"Thank you." Mr. Defender let his mild, guileless gaze roam over the court. There was nothing in his plump features to warn them of the coming wallop. In quieter tones, he asked. "Male or female?"

"Female," said Allain.

A reporter dropped a book. That was the only sound for most of a minute. Then came a deep indrawn hiss of breath, a rapid ticking as cameras traversed to focus on Maeth, a running murmur of surprise from one end of the court to the other.

Back of the gallery, the most pungent cartoonist of the day tore up his latest effort, a sketch of defendant strapped to a rocket hell-bent for the Moon. It was captioned, "Spike's Hike."

What could one call it—him—*her*, now? Spikina? He raked his hair, sought a new tack, knowing that there was none. You just can't crucify a small and lonely female.

Mr. Prosecutor sat with firmed lips and the fatalistic air of one who has had eighty percent of the ground snatched from under his feet. He knew his public. He could estimate their reaction to within ten thousand votes, plus or minus.

All stared at the golden eyes. They were still large, but somehow had become soft and luminous in a way not noticed before. You could see that now. Having been told, you could really *see* that they were feminine. And in some peculiar, inexplicable manner the outlines around them had become subdued, less outlandish, even vaguely and remotely human!

With effective technique, the defending attorney gave them plenty of time to stew their thoughts before carefully he struck again.

"Your Honors, there is one witness for my side."

Mr. Prosecutor rocked back, stared searchingly around the court. The judges polished their glasses, looked around also. One of them motioned to a court official who promptly bawled in stentorian tones.

"Defense witness!"

It shuttled around the great room in echoing murmurs. "Defense witness! There is a witness for the defense!"

A bald-headed little man came self-conciously from the public section, bearing a large envelope. Reaching the chair, he did not take it himself, but instead placed upon it a photograph blown up to four feet by three.

Court and cameras gave the picture no more than the briefest glance, for it was instantly recognizable. A lady holding a lamp.

Rising with a disapproving frown, the prosecuting attorney complained, "Your Honors, if my learned opponent is permitted to treat the Statue of Liberty as a witness he will thereby bring into ridicule the proceedings of this—"

A judge waved him down with the acid comment, "The bench is fully capable of asserting the dignity of this court." He shifted his attention to Mr. Defender, eyeing him over the tops of his glasses. "A witness may be defined as one able to assist the jury in arriving at a just conclusion."

"I am aware of that, Your Honor," assured Mr. Defender, not in the least disturbed.

"Very well." The judge leaned back, slightly baffled. "Let the court hear witness's statement."

Mr. Defender signed to the little man, who immediately produced another large photograph and placed it over the first.

This was of the enormous plinth, with Liberty's bronze skirt drapes barely visible at its top. There were words on the plinth, written bold and large. Some in the court gave the picture only another swift look, since they knew the words by heart, but others read them right through, once, twice, even three times.

Many had never seen the words before, including some who had passed nearby them twice daily, for years. Cameras picked up the words, transmitted them pictorially to millions to whom they were new. An announcer recited them over the radio.

> Give me your tired, your poor,
> Your huddled masses yearning to breathe free,

The wretched refuse of your teeming shore.
Send these, the homeless, tempest-tossed, to me,
I lift my lamp beside the golden door!

In the deep, heart-searching silence that followed, nobody noticed that Mr. Defender had bowed deeply to the judges and resumed his seat. The defense rested, having nothing more to add.

Midnight. A large stone cell with a metal grille, a bed, a table, two chairs, and a radio in one corner. Maeth and the plump man sat there conversing, examining correspondence, watching the clock.

"The opposition picked a sloppy one with that crackpot's letter," remarked Mr. Defender. He could not refrain from expressing himself vocally though he knew full well that the other was hearing only the thoughts within his mind. He tapped a heavy forefinger on the bunch of missives at which they had been looking. "I could easily have countered him with this bunch written from a week ago to way back. But what was the use? They prove nothing except that all people don't think alike."

He sighed, stretched his arms wide and yawned, had his twentieth or thirtieth look at the clock, picked up another letter. "Listen to this one." He read it aloud.

"My son, aged thirteen, keeps pestering us to offer your client a home for at least a little while. I really don't know whether we are being wise in giving way to him, but we shall certainly suffer if we don't. We have a spare room here, and

68

if your client is clean about the house and don't mind a bit of steam around on wash-days—"

His voice petered out as he had to yawn again. "They say it will be six in the morning before this public poll is complete. Bet you it's at least eight o'clock and maybe ten. They're always late with these things." He jerked around in a vain effort to make himself more comfortable in his hard chair. "However, I'm staying with you until we've seen this through, one way or the other. And don't kid yourself I'm the only friend you've got." He pointed to the letters. "You've plenty there, and none of them certifiable."

Maeth ceased perusal of a note in uneven, spidery writing, reached for pencil and paper and scribbled, "Allain did not teach me enough words. What is a 'veteran'?" Having had it explained, she said, "I like this writer best. He has been hurt. If I am freed I will accept his invitation."

"Let me see." Taking the note, Mr. Defender read it, murmuring, "Um . . . um . . ." as he went along. He handed it back. "The choice is yours. You'll have something in common, anyway, since you'll both be coping with a cockeyed world." Throwing a glance at the wall, he added, "That clock has gone into a crawl. It's going to take us a week to get to morning."

Somebody opened the grille with a jangle of keys, and Mr. Prosecutor came in. Grinning at his rival, he said, "Al, you sure make it tough for yourself in the clink—you don't even use the comforts provided."

"Meaning what?"

"The radio."

Mr. Defender gave a disdainful sniff. "Darn the radio. Noise, noise, noise. We've been busy reading—in peace and quiet." Sudden suspicion flooded his ample features. "What have we missed on the radio, if anything?"

"The midnight news." Mr. Prosecutor leaned on the edge of the table, still grinning. "They have thrown up the poll."

"They can't do that!" The defending attorney stood up, flushed with anger. "It was by international agreement that this case was—"

"They can do it in certain circumstances," interrupted the other, "which are that a torrent of votes overwhelmingly in favor of your client has already made further counting a waste of time." He turned to Maeth, finished, "Just between you and me, Funny-face, I was never more happy to lose a fight."

The man in the back room was nearing middle age, prematurely gray, and had long slender fingers that were sensitive tools. He was listening to the radio when the doorbell rang. There was no video in the room, only the radio softly playing a Polynesian melody. The bell jarred through the music, causing him to switch off and come upright. Very deliberately he moved around the room, through the door and into the passage.

Strange for anyone to call in the early evening. Not often that people came then. The mailman occasionally turned up in the morning and one or two tradesmen toward midday. Rarely did somebody appear later, all too rarely. He was not expecting a visitor, either.

He trod gently along the passage toward the front door, his feet silent on the thick carpet, his right hand brushing the wall.

There was something mighty queer about this summons because as he neared the door he conceived the weird notion that he knew in advance who was waiting outside. The picture crept into his mind, shadowy but discernible, as if insinuated by some means he could not define, as if hopefully projected by one of those beyond the door. It was a picture of a big, plump, confident man accompanied by something small, all green and golden.

Despite past trials and stern testings which had made him what he was today, his nerves were passably good and he was not subject to delusions, or had not yet developed a tendency to delusions. So he was puzzled, even a little upset by preconceptions without any basis. He had never known a big, heavy man such as his brain was picturing, not even in other more normal days. As for the second one . . .

Here and there, of course, are people with greatly sharpened senses, with odd aptitudes developed to an extreme. That was to be expected, for the fates were kind and provided compensation. Without them, it would be hard to get around. But he knew his own and they included none like this.

His fingers, usually so precise, fumbled badly as they sought the door-latch, almost as if they had temporarily forgotten where it was placed. Then, finding it, they began to turn the lock, and at that point a thin piping voice came into his mind as clearly as a tinkling bell.

"Open please—*I am your eyes!*"

Frank Belknap Long

The Mississippi
Saucer

> *Here is a charming picture of our heartland.*
> *It emphasizes bravery and the virtues*
> *of being a soarhead.*

Jimmy watched the *Natchez Belle* draw near, a shining eagerness in his stare. He stood on the deck of the shantyboat, his toes sticking out of his socks, his heart knocking against his ribs. Straight down the river the big packet boat came, purpling the water with its shadow, its smokestacks belching soot.

Jimmy had a wild talent for collecting things. He knew exactly how to infuriate the captains without sticking out his neck. Up and down the Father of Waters, from the bayous of Louisiana to the Great Sandy, other little shantyboat boys envied Jimmy and tried hard to imitate him.

But Jimmy had a very special gift, a genius for pantomime.

He'd wait until there was a glimmer of red flame on the river and small objects stood out with a startling clarity. Then he'd go into his act.

Nothing upset the captains quite so much as Jimmy's habit of holding a big, croaking bullfrog up by its legs as the riverboats went steaming past. It was a surefire way of reminding the captains that men and frogs were brothers under the skin. The puffed-out throat of the frog told the captains exactly what Jimmy thought of their cheek.

Jimmy refrained from making faces, or sticking out his tongue at the grinning roustabouts. It was the frog that did the trick.

In the still dawn, things came sailing Jimmy's way, hurled by captains with a twinkle of repressed merriment dancing in eyes that were kindlier and more tolerant than Jimmy dreamed.

Just because shantyboat folk had no right to insult the riverboats Jimmy had collected forty empty tobacco tins, a down-at-heels shoe, a Sears Roebuck catalogue, and more rolled-up newspapers than Jimmy could ever read.

Jimmy could read, of course. No matter how badly Uncle Al needed a new pair of shoes, Jimmy's education came first. So Jimmy had spent six winters ashore in a first-class grammar school, his books paid for out of Uncle Al's "New Orleans" money.

Uncle Al, blowing on a vinegar jug and making sweet music, the holes in his socks much bigger than the holes in Jimmy's socks. Uncle Al shaking his head and saying sadly, "Some day, young fella, I ain't gonna sit here harmonizing. No siree! I'm gonna buy myself a brand-new store suit, trade in this here jig jug for a big round banjo, and hie myself off to the Mardi

Gras. Ain't too old thataway to git a little fun out of life, young fella!"

Poor old Uncle Al. The money he'd saved up for the Mardi Gras never seemed to stretch far enough. There was enough kindness in him to stretch like a rainbow over the bayous and the river forests of sweet, rustling pine for as far as the eye could see. Enough kindness to wrap all of Jimmy's life in a glow, and the life of Jimmy's sister as well.

Jimmy's parents had died of winter pneumonia too soon to appreciate Uncle Al. But up and down the river everyone knew that Uncle Al was a great man.

Enemies? Well, sure, all great men made enemies, didn't they?

The Harmon brothers were downright sinful about carrying their feuding meanness right up to the doorstep of Uncle Al, if it could be said that a man living in a shantyboat had a doorstep.

Uncle Al made big catches and the Harmon brothers never seemed to have any luck. So, long before Jimmy was old enough to understand how corrosive envy could be, the Harmon brothers had started feuding with Uncle Al.

"Jimmy, here comes the *Natchez Belle*! Uncle Al says for you to get him a newspaper. The newspaper you got him yesterday he couldn't read no-ways. It was soaking wet!"

Jimmy turned to glower at his sister. Up and down the river Pigtail Anne was known as a tomboy, but she wasn't—no-ways. She was Jimmy's little sister. That meant Jimmy was the man in the family, and wore the pants, and nothing Pigtail said or did could change that for one minute.

"Don't yell at me!" Jimmy complained. "How can I get Captain Simmons mad if you get me mad first? Have a heart, will you?"

But Pigtail Anne refused to budge. Even when the *Natchez Belle* loomed so close to the shantyboat that it blotted out the sky, she continued to crowd her brother, preventing him from holding up the frog and making Captain Simmons squirm.

But Jimmy got the newspaper anyway. Captain Simmons had a keen insight into tomboy psychology, and from the bridge of the *Natchez Belle* he could see that Pigtail was making life miserable for Jimmy.

True—Jimmy had no respect for packet boats and deserved a good trouncing. But what a scrapper the lad was! Never let it be said that in a struggle between the sexes the men of the river did not stand shoulder to shoulder.

The paper came sailing over the shining brown water like a white-bellied buffalo cat shot from a sling.

Pigtail grabbed it before Jimmy could give her a shove. Calmly she unwrapped it, her chin tilted in bellicose defiance.

As the *Natchez Belle* dwindled around a lazy, cypress-shadowed bend, Pigtail Anne became a superior being, wrapped in a cosmopolitan aura. A wide-eyed little girl on a swaying deck, the great outside world rushing straight toward her from all directions.

Pigtail could take that world in her stride. She liked the fashion page best, but she was not above clicking her tongue at everything in the paper.

"Kidnap plot linked to airliner crash killing fifty," she read. "Red Sox blank Yanks! Congress sits today, vowing vengeance!

75

Million-dollar heiress elopes with a clerk! Court lets dog pick owner! Girl of eight kills her brother in accidental shooting!"

"I ought to push your face right down in the mud," Jimmy muttered.

"Don't you dare! I've a right to see what's going on in the world!"

"You said the paper was for Uncle Al!"

"It is—when I get finished with it."

Jimmy started to take hold of his sister's wrist and pry the paper from her clasp. Only started—for as Pigtail wriggled back, sunlight fell on a shadowed part of the paper which drew Jimmy's gaze as sunlight draws dew.

Exciting wasn't the word for the headline. It seemed to blaze out of the page at Jimmy as he stared, his chin nudging Pigtail's shoulder.

NEW FLYING MONSTER REPORTED
BLAZING GULF STATE SKIES

Jimmy snatched the paper and backed away from Pigtail, his eyes glued to the headline.

He was kind to his sister, however. He read the news item aloud, if an account so startling could be called an item. To Jimmy, it seemed more like a dazzling burst of light in the sky.

"A New Orleans resident reported today that he saw a big bright object, 'roundish like a disk,' flying north, against the wind. 'It was all lighted up from inside!' the observer stated. 'As far as I could tell there were no signs of life aboard the thing. It was much bigger than any of the flying saucers previously reported!'"

"People keep seeing them!" Jimmy muttered, after a pause. "Nobody knows where they come from! Saucers flying through the sky, high up at night. In the daytime, too! Maybe we're being *watched*, Pigtail!"

"Watched? Jimmy, what do you mean? What you talking about?"

Jimmy stared at his sister, the paper jiggling in his clasp. "It's way over your head, Pigtail!" he said sympathetically. "I'll prove it! What's a planet?"

"A star in the sky, you dope!" Pigtail almost screamed. "Wait'll Uncle Al hears what a meanie you are. If I wasn't your sister you wouldn't dare grab a paper that doesn't belong to you."

Jimmy refused to be enraged. "A planet's not a star, Pigtail," he said patiently. "A star's a big ball of fire like the sun. A planet is small and cool, like the Earth. Some of the planets may even have people on them. Not people like us, but people all the same. Maybe we're just frogs to them!"

"You're crazy, Jimmy! Crazy, crazy, you hear?"

Jimmy started to reply, then shut his mouth tight. Big waves were nothing new in the wake of steamboats, but the shanty-boat wasn't just riding a swell. It was swaying and rocking like a floating barrel in the kind of blow shantyboaters dreaded worse than the thought of dying.

Jimmy knew that a big blow could come up fast. Straight down from the sky in gusts, from all directions, banging against the boat like a drunken roustabout, slamming doors, tearing away mooring planks.

The river could rise fast too. Under the lashing of a hurricane blowing up from the gulf, the river could lift a shantyboat right out of the water, and smash it to smithereens against a tree.

But now the blow was coming from just one part of the sky. A funnel of wind was churning the river into a white froth and raising big swells directly offshore. But the river wasn't rising and the sun was shining in a clear sky.

Jimmy knew a dangerous floodwater storm when he saw one. The sky had to be dark with rain, and you had to feel scared, in fear of drowning.

Jimmy was scared, all right. That part of it rang true. But a hollow, sick feeling in his chest couldn't mean anything by itself, he told himself fiercely.

Pigtail Anne saw the disk before Jimmy did. She screamed and pointed skyward, her twin braids standing straight out in the wind like the ropes on a bale of cotton when smokestacks collapse and a savage howling sends the river ghosts scurrying for cover.

Straight down out of the sky the disk swooped, a huge, spinning shape as flat as a buckwheat cake swimming in a golden haze of butterfat.

But the disk didn't remind Jimmy of a buckwheat cake. It made him think instead of a slowly turning wheel in the pilot house of a rotting old riverboat, a big, ghostly wheel manned by a steersman a century dead, his eyesockets filled with flickering swamp lights.

It made Jimmy want to run and hide. Almost it made him want to cling to his sister, content to let her wear the pants if only he could be spared the horror.

For there was something so chilling about the down-sweeping disk that Jimmy's heart began leaping like a vinegar jug bobbing about in the wake of a capsizing fishboat.

Lower and lower the disk swept, trailing plumes of white smoke, lashing the water with a fearful blow. Straight down over the cypress wilderness that fringed the opposite bank, and then out across the river with a long-drawn whistling sound, louder than the air-sucking death gasps of a thousand buffalo cats.

Jimmy didn't see the disk strike the shining broad shoulders of the Father of Waters, for the bend around which the *Natchez Belle* had steamed so proudly hid the sky monster from view. But Jimmy did see the waterspout, spiraling skyward like the atom bomb explosion he'd goggled at in the pages of an old *Life* magazine, all smudged now with oily thumbprints.

Just a roaring for an instant—and a big white mushroom shooting straight up into the sky. Then, slowly, the mushroom decayed and fell back, and an awful stillness settled down over the river.

The stillness was broken by a shrill cry from Pigtail Anne. "It was a flying saucer! Jimmy, we've seen one! We've seen one! We've—"

"Shut your mouth, Pigtail!"

Jimmy shaded his eyes and stared out across the river, his chest a throbbing ache.

He was still staring when a door creaked behind him.

Jimmy trembled. A tingling fear went through him, for he found it hard to realize that the disk had swept around the bend out of sight. To his overheated imagination it continued to fill all of the sky above him, overshadowing the shantyboat, making every sound a threat.

Sucking the still air deep into his lungs, Jimmy swung about.

Uncle Al was standing on the deck in a little pool of sunlight, his gaunt, hollow-cheeked face set in harsh lines. Uncle Al was shading his eyes, too. But he was staring up the river, not down.

"Trouble, young fella," he grunted. "Sure as I'm a-standin' here. A barrelful o' trouble—headin' straight for us!"

Jimmy gulped and gestured wildly toward the bend. "It came down *over there*, Uncle Al!" he got out. "Pigtail saw it, too! A big, flying—"

"The Harmons are a-comin', young fella," Uncle Al drawled, silencing Jimmy with a wave of his hand. "Yesterday I rowed over a Harmon jug line without meanin' to. Now Jed Harmon's tellin' everybody I stole his fish!"

Very calmly Uncle Al cut himself a slice of the strongest tobacco on the river and packed it carefully in his pipe, wadding it down with his thumb.

He started to put the pipe between his teeth, then thought better of it.

"I can bone-feel the Harmon boat a-comin', young fella," he said, using the pipe to gesture with. "Smooth and quiet over the river like a moccasin snake."

Jimmy turned pale. He forgot about the disk and the mushrooming waterspout. When he shut his eyes he saw only a red haze overhanging the river, and a shantyboat nosing out of the cypresses, its windows spitting death.

Jimmy knew that the Harmons had waited a long time for an excuse. The Harmons were law-respecting river rats with

80

sharp teeth. Feuding wasn't lawful, but murder could be made lawful by whittling down a lie until it looked as sharp as the truth.

The Harmon brothers would do their whittling down with double-barreled shotguns. It was easy enough to make murder look like a lawful crime if you could point to a body covered by a blanket and say, "We caught him stealing our fish! He was a-goin' to kill us—so we got him first."

No one would think of lifting the blanket and asking Uncle Al about it. A man lying stiff and still under a blanket could no more make himself heard than a river cat frozen in the ice.

"Git inside, young 'uns. *Here they come!*"

Jimmy's heart skipped a beat. Down the river in the sunlight a shantyboat was drifting. Jimmy could see the Harmon brothers crouching on the deck, their faces livid with hate, sunlight glinting on their arm-cradled shotguns.

The Harmon brothers were not in the least alike. Jed Harmon was tall and gaunt, his right cheek puckered by a knife scar, his cruel, thin-lipped mouth snagged by his teeth. Joe Harmon was small and stout, a little round man with bushy eyebrows and the flabby face of a cottonmouth snake.

"Go inside, Pigtail," Jimmy said, calmly. "I'm a-goin' to stay and fight!"

Uncle Al grabbed Jimmy's arm and swung him around. "You heard what I said, young fella. Now git!"

"I want to stay here and fight with you, Uncle Al," Jimmy said.

"Have you got a gun? Do you want to be blown apart, young fella?"

"I'm not scared, Uncle Al," Jimmy pleaded. "You might get wounded. I know how to shoot straight, Uncle Al. If you get hurt I'll go right on fighting!"

"No you won't, young fella! Take Pigtail inside. You hear me? You want me to take you across my knee and beat the livin' stuffings out of you?"

Silence.

Deep in his uncle's face Jimmy saw an anger he couldn't buck. Grabbing Pigtail Anne by the arm, he propelled her across the deck and into the dismal front room of the shanty-boat.

The instant he released her she glared at him and stamped her foot. "If Uncle Al gets shot it'll be your fault," she said cruelly. Then Pigtail's anger really flared up.

"The Harmons wouldn't dare shoot us 'cause we're children!"

For an instant brief as a dropped heartbeat Jimmy stared at his sister with unconcealed admiration.

"You can be right smart when you've got nothing else on your mind, Pigtail," he said. "If they kill me they'll hang sure as shooting!"

Jimmy was out in the sunlight again before Pigtail could make a grab for him.

Out on the deck and running along the deck toward Uncle Al. He was still running when the first blast came.

It didn't sound like a shotgun blast. The deck shook and a big swirl of smoke floated straight toward Jimmy, half blinding him and blotting Uncle Al from view.

When the smoke cleared Jimmy could see the Harmon

shantyboat. It was less than thirty feet away now, drifting straight past and rocking with the tide like a topheavy flatbarge.

On the deck Jed Harmon was crouching down, his gaunt face split in a triumphant smirk. Beside him Joe Harmon stood quivering like a mound of jelly, a stick of dynamite in his hand, his flabby face looking almost gentle in the slanting sunlight.

There was a little square box at Jed Harmon's feet. As Joe pitched, Jed reached into the box for another dynamite stick. Jed was passing the sticks along to his brother, depending on wad dynamite to silence Uncle Al forever.

Wildly Jimmy told himself that the guns had been just a trick to mix Uncle Al up, and keep him from shooting until they had him where they wanted him.

Uncle Al was shooting now, his face as grim as death. His big heavy gun was leaping about like mad, almost hurling him to the deck.

Jimmy saw the second dynamite stick spinning through the air, but he never saw it come down. All he could see was the smoke and the shantyboat rocking, and there was another terrible splintering crash as he went plunging into the river from the end of a rising plank, a sob strangling in his throat.

Jimmy struggled up from the river with the long leg thrusts of a terrified bullfrog, his head a throbbing ache. As he swam shoreward he could see the cypresses on the opposite bank, dark against the sun, and something that looked like the roof of a house with water washing over it.

Then, with mud sucking at his heels, Jimmy was clinging

to a slippery bank and staring out across the river, shading his eyes against the glare.

Jimmy thought, "I'm dreaming! I'll wake up and see Uncle Joe blowing on a vinegar jug. I'll see Pigtail, too. Uncle Al will be sitting on the deck, taking it easy!"

But Uncle Al wasn't sitting on the deck. There was no deck for Uncle Al to sit upon. Just the top of the shantyboat, sinking lower and lower, and Uncle Al swimming.

Uncle Al had his arm around Pigtail, and Jimmy could see Pigtail's white face bobbing up and down as Uncle Al breasted the tide with his strong right arm.

Closer to the bend was the Harmon shantyboat. The Harmons were using their shotguns now, blasting fiercely away at Uncle Al and Pigtail. Jimmy could see the smoke curling up from the leaping guns and the water jumping up and down in little spurts all about Uncle Al.

There was an awful hollow agony in Jimmy's chest as he stared, a fear that was partly a soundless screaming and partly a vision of Uncle Al sinking down through the dark water and turning it red.

It was strange, though. Something was happening to Jimmy, nibbling away at the outer edges of the fear like a big, hungry river cat. Making the fear seem less swollen and awful, shredding it away in little flakes.

There was a white core of anger in Jimmy which seemed suddenly to blaze up.

He shut his eyes tight.

In his mind's gaze Jimmy saw himself holding the Harmon brothers up by their long, mottled legs. The Harmon brothers were frogs. Not friendly, good-natured frogs like Uncle Al, but snake frogs. Cottonmouth frogs.

All flannel red were their mouths, and they had long evil fangs which dripped poison in the sunlight. But Jimmy wasn't afraid of them no-ways. Not anymore. He had too firm a grip on their legs.

"Don't let anything happen to Uncle Al and Pigtail!" Jimmy whispered, as though he were talking to himself. No—not exactly to himself. To someone like himself, only larger. Very close to Jimmy, but larger, more powerful.

"Catch them before they harm Uncle Al! Hurry! *Hurry!*"

There was a strange lifting sensation in Jimmy's chest now. As though he could shake the river if he tried hard enough, tilt it, send it swirling in great thunderous white surges clear down to Lake Pontchartrain.

But Jimmy didn't want to tilt the river. Not with Uncle Al on it and Pigtail, and all those people in New Orleans who would disappear right off the streets. They were frogs, too, maybe, but good frogs. Not like the Harmon brothers.

Jimmy had a funny picture of himself much younger than he was. Jimmy saw himself as a great husky baby, standing in the middle of the river and blowing on it with all his might. The waves rose and rose, and Jimmy's cheeks swelled out and the river kept getting angrier.

No—he must fight that.

"Save Uncle Al!" he whispered fiercely. "Just save him—and Pigtail!"

It began to happen the instant Jimmy opened his eyes.

Around the bend in the sunlight came a great spinning disk, wrapped in a fiery glow.

Straight toward the Harmon shantyboat the disk swept, water spurting up all about it, its bottom fifty feet wide. There was no collision. Only a brightness for one awful instant where the shantyboat was twisting and turning in the current, a brightness that outshone the rising sun.

Just like a camera flashbulb going off, but bigger, brighter. So big and bright that Jimmy could see the faces of the Harmon brothers fifty times as large as life, shriveling and disappearing in a magnifying burst of flame high above the cypress trees. Just as though a giant in the sky had trained a big burning glass on the Harmon brothers and whipped it back quick.

Whipped it straight up, so that the faces would grow huge before dissolving as a warning to all snakes. There was an evil anguish in the dissolving faces which made Jimmy's blood run cold. Then the disk was alone in the middle of the river, spinning around and around, the shantyboat swallowed up.

And Uncle Al was still swimming, fearfully close to it.

The net came swirling out of the disk over Uncle Al like a great, dew-drenched gossamer web. It enmeshed him as he swam, so gently that he hardly seemed to struggle or even to be aware of what was happening to him.

Pigtail didn't resist, either. She simply stopped thrashing in Uncle Al's arms, as though a great wonder had come upon her.

Slowly Uncle Al and Pigtail were drawn into the disk. Jimmy could see Uncle Al reclining in the web, with Pigtail in the crook of his arm, his long, angular body as quiet as a butterfly in its deep winter sleep inside a swaying glass cocoon.

Uncle Al and Pigtail, being drawn together into the disk as Jimmy stared, a dull pounding in his chest. After a moment the pounding subsided and a silence settled down over the river.

Jimmy sucked in his breath. The voices began quietly, as though they had been waiting for a long time to speak to Jimmy deep inside his head, and didn't want to frighten him in any way.

"Take it easy, Jimmy! Stay where you are. We're just going to have a friendly little talk with Uncle Al."

"A t-talk?" Jimmy heard himself stammering.

"We knew we'd find you where life flows simply and serenely, Jimmy. Your parents took care of that before they left you with Uncle Al.

"You see, Jimmy, we wanted you to study the Earth people on a great, wide flowing river, far from the cruel, twisted places. To grow up with them, Jimmy—and to understand them. Especially the Uncle Als. For Uncle Al is unspoiled, Jimmy. If there's any hope at all for Earth as we guide and watch it, that hope burns most brightly in the Uncle Als!"

The voice paused, then went on quickly. "You see, Jimmy, you're not human in the same way that your sister is human— or Uncle Al. But you're still young enough to feel human, and we want you to feel human, Jimmy."

"W-who are you?" Jimmy gasped.

"We are the Shining Ones, Jimmy! For wide wastes of years we have cruised Earth's skies, almost unnoticed by the Earth people. When darkness wraps the Earth in a great, spinning shroud we hide our ships close to the cities, and glide through the silent streets in search of our young. You see, Jimmy, we must watch and protect the young of our race until sturdiness comes upon them, and they are ready for the Great Change."

For an instant there was a strange, humming sound deep inside Jimmy's head, like the drowsy murmur of bees in a dew-drenched clover patch. Then the voice droned on. "The Earth people are frightened by our ships now, for their cruel wars have put a great fear of death in their hearts. They watch the skies with sharper eyes, and their minds have groped closer to the truth.

"To the Earth people our ships are no longer the fireballs of mysterious legend, haunted will-o'-the-wisps, marsh flickerings and the even more illusive distortions of the sick in mind. It is a long bold step from fireballs to flying saucers, Jimmy. A day will come when the Earth people will be wise enough to put aside fear. Then we can show ourselves to them as we really are, and help them openly."

The voice seemed to take more complete possession of Jimmy's thoughts then, growing louder and more eager, echoing through his mind with the persuasiveness of muted chimes.

"Jimmy, close your eyes tight. We're going to take you across wide gulfs of space to the bright and shining land of your birth."

Jimmy obeyed.

It was a city, and yet it wasn't like New York or Chicago or any of the other cities Jimmy had seen illustrations of in the newspapers and picture magazines.

The buildings were white and domed and shining, and they seemed to tower straight up into the sky. There were streets too, weaving in and out between the domes like rainbow-colored spider webs in a forest of mushrooms.

There were no people in the city, but down the aerial streets shining objects swirled with the swift, easy gliding of flat stones skimming an edge of running water.

Then as Jimmy stared into the depths of the strange glow behind his eyelids, the city dwindled and fell away, and he saw a huge circular disk looming in a wilderness of shadows. Straight toward the disk a shining object moved, bearing aloft on filaments of flame a much smaller object that struggled and mewed and reached out little white arms.

Closer and closer the shining object came, until Jimmy could see that it was carrying a human infant that stared straight at Jimmy out of wide, dark eyes. But before he could get a really good look at the shining object, it pierced the shadows and passed into the disk.

There was a sudden, blinding burst of light, and the disk was gone.

Jimmy opened his eyes.

"You were once like that baby, Jimmy!" the voice said. "You were carried by your parents into a waiting ship, and then out across wide gulfs of space to Earth.

"You see, Jimmy, our race was once entirely human. But as we grew to maturity we left the warm little worlds where our infancy was spent, and boldly sought the stars, shedding our humanness as sunlight sheds the dew, or a bright, soaring moth of the night its ugly pupa case.

"We grew great and wise, Jimmy, but not quite wise enough to shed our human heritage of love and joy and heartbreak.

In our childhood we must return to the scenes of our past, to take root again in familiar soil, to grow in power and wisdom slowly and sturdily, like a seed dropped back into the loam which nourished the great flowering mother plant.

"Or like the eel of Earth's seas, Jimmy, that must be spawned in the depths of the great cold ocean, and swim slowly back to the bright highlands and the shining rivers of Earth. Young eels do not resemble their parents, Jimmy. They're white and thin and transparent and have to struggle hard to survive and grow up.

"Jimmy, you were planted here by your parents to grow wise and strong. Deep in your mind you knew that we had come to seek you out, for we are all born human, and are bound one to another by that knowledge, and that secret trust.

"You knew that we would watch over you and see that no harm would come to you. You called out to us, Jimmy, with all the strength of your mind and heart. Your Uncle Al was in danger and you sensed our nearness.

"It was partly your knowledge that saved him, Jimmy. But it took courage too, and a willingness to believe that you were more than human, and armed with the great proud strength and wisdom of the Shining Ones."

The voice grew suddenly gentle, like a caressing wind.

"You're not old enough yet to go home, Jimmy! Or wise enough. We'll take you home when the time comes. Now we just want to have a talk with Uncle Al, to find out how you're getting along."

Jimmy looked down into the river and then up into the sky. Deep down under the dark, swirling water he could see life taking shape in a thousand forms. Caddis flies building bright, shining new nests, and dragonfly nymphs crawling up toward the sunlight, and pollywogs growing sturdy hind limbs to conquer the land.

But there were cottonmouths down there too, with death behind their fangs, and no love for the life that was crawling upward. When Jimmy looked up into the sky he could see all the blazing stars of space, with cottonmouths on every planet of every sun.

Uncle Al was like a bright caddis fly building a fine new nest, thatched with kindness, denying himself bright little Mardi Gras pleasures so that Jimmy could go to school and grow wiser than Uncle Al.

"That's right, Jimmy. You're growing up—we can see that! Uncle Al says he told you to hide from the cottonmouths. But you were ready to give your life for your sister and Uncle Al."

"Shucks, it was nothing!" Jimmy heard himself protesting.

"Uncle Al doesn't think so. And neither do we!"

A long silence while the river mists seemed to weave a bright cocoon of radiance about Jimmy clinging to the bank, and the great circular disk that had swallowed up Uncle Al.

Then the voices began again. "No reason why Uncle Al shouldn't have a little fun out of life, Jimmy. Gold's easy to make and we'll make some right now. A big lump of gold in Uncle Al's hand won't hurt him in any way."

"Whenever he gets any spending money he gives it away!" Jimmy gulped.

"I know, Jimmy. But he'll listen to you. Tell him you want to go to New Orleans too!"

Jimmy looked up quickly then. In his heart was something of the wonder he'd felt when he'd seen his first riverboat and waited for he knew not what. Something of the wonder that must have come to men seeking magic in the sky, the rain-makers of ancient tribes and of days long vanished.

Only to Jimmy the wonder came now with a white burst of remembrance and recognition.

It was as though he could sense something of himself in the two towering spheres that rose straight up out of the water behind the disk. Still and white and beautiful they were, like bubbles floating on a rainbow sea with all the stars of space behind them.

Staring at them, Jimmy saw himself as he would be, and knew himself for what he was. It was not a glory to be long endured.

"Now you must forget again, Jimmy! Forget as Uncle Al will forget—until we come for you. Be a little shantyboat boy! You are safe on the wide bosom of the Father of Waters. Your parents planted you in a rich and kindly loam, and in all the finite universes you will find no cozier nook, for life flows here with a diversity that is infinite and—*Pigtail*! She gets on your nerves at times, doesn't she, Jimmy?"

"She sure does," Jimmy admitted.

"Be patient with her, Jimmy. She's the only human sister you'll ever have on Earth."

"I—I'll try!" Jimmy muttered.

Uncle Al and Pigtail came out of the disk in an amazingly simple way. They just seemed to float out, in the glimmering web. Then, suddenly, there wasn't any disk on the river at all—just a dull flickering where the sky had opened like a great, blazing furnace to swallow it up.

"I was just swimmin' along with Pigtail, not worryin' too much, 'cause there's no sense in worryin' when death is starin' you in the face," Uncle Al muttered, a few minutes later.

Uncle Al sat on the riverbank beside Jimmy, staring down at his palm, his vision misted a little by a furious blinking.

"It's gold, Uncle Al!" Pigtail shrilled. "A big lump of solid gold—"

"I just felt my hand get heavy and there it was, young fella, nestling there in my palm!"

Jimmy didn't seem to be able to say anything.

"High school books don't cost no more than grammar school books, young fella," Uncle Al said, his face a sudden shining. "Next winter you'll be a-goin' to high school, sure as I'm sittin' here!"

For a moment the sunlight seemed to blaze so brightly about Uncle Al that Jimmy couldn't even see the holes in his socks.

Then Uncle Al made a wry face. "Someday, young fella, when your books are all paid for, I'm gonna buy myself a brand-new store suit, and hie myself off to the Mardi Gras. Ain't too old thataway to git a little fun out of life, young fella!"

R. A. *Lafferty*

Primary Education
of the Camiroi

*You think school is tough right now? Wait
till you see the suggestions made in this story.*

ABSTRACT FROM JOINT REPORT TO THE GENERAL DUBUQUE
PTA CONCERNING THE PRIMARY EDUCATION OF THE CAMIROI;
Subtitled: Critical Observations of a Parallel Culture on a
Neighboring World, and Evaluations of the Other Way of
Education.

EXTRACT FROM THE DAY BOOK:

"Where," we asked the Information Factor at Camiroi City
Terminal, "is the office of the local PTA?"

"Isn't any," he said cheerfully.

"You mean that in Camiroi City, the metropolis of the
planet, there is no PTA?" our chairman, Paul Piper, asked
with disbelief.

"Isn't any office of it. But you're poor strangers, so you deserve an answer even if you can't frame your questions properly. See that elderly man sitting on the bench and enjoying the sun? Go tell him you need a PTA. He'll make you one."

"Perhaps the initials convey a different meaning on Camiroi," said Miss Munch, the first surrogate chairman. "By them we mean—"

"Parent Teachers Apparatus, of course. Colloquial English is one of the six Earthian languages required here, you know. Don't be abashed. He's a fine person, and he enjoys doing things for strangers. He'll be glad to make you a PTA."

We were nonplussed, but we walked over to the man indicated.

"We are looking for the local PTA, sir," said Miss Smice, our second surrogate chairman. "We were told you might help us."

"Oh, certainly," said the elderly Camiroi gentleman. "One of you arrest that man walking there, and we'll get started with it."

"Do what?" asked our Mr. Piper.

"Arrest him. I have noticed that your own words sometimes do not convey a meaning to you. I often wonder how you do communicate among yourselves. Arrest, take into custody, seize by any force physical or moral, and bring him here."

"Yes, *sir*," cried Miss Hanks, our third surrogate chairman. She enjoyed things like this. She arrested the walking Camiroi man with force partly physical and partly moral and brought him to the group.

"It's a PTA they want, Meander," the elder Camiroi said

to the one arrested. "Grab three more, and we'll get started. Let the lady help. She's good at it."

Our Miss Hanks and the Camiroi man named Meander arrested three other Camiroi men and brought them to the group.

"Five. It's enough," said the elderly Camiroi. "We are hereby constituted a PTA and ordered into random action. Now, how can we accommodate you, good Earth people?"

"But are you legal? Are you five persons competent to be a PTA?" demanded our Mr. Piper.

"Any Camiroi citizen is competent to do any job on the planet of Camiroi," said one of the Camiroi men (we learned later that his name was Talarium), "otherwise Camiroi would be in a sad shape."

"It may be," said our Miss Smice sourly. "It all seems very informal. What if one of you had to be World President?"

"The odds are that it won't come to one man in ten," said the elderly Camiroi (his name was Philoxenus). "I'm the only one of this group ever to serve as president of this planet, and it was a pleasant week I spent in the Office. Now to the point. How can we accommodate you?"

"We would like to see one of your schools in session," said our Mr. Piper. "We would like to talk to the teachers and the students. We are here to compare the two systems of education."

"There is no comparison," said old Philoxenus, "meaning no offense. Or no more than a little. On Camiroi, we practice Education. On Earth, they play a game, but they call it by the same name. That makes the confusion. Come. We'll go to a school in session."

"And to a public school," said Miss Smice suspiciously. "Do not fob off any fancy private school on us as typical."

"That would be difficult," said Philoxenus. "There is no public school in Camiroi City and only two remaining on the Planet. Only a small fraction of one percent of the students of Camiroi are in public schools. We maintain that there is no more reason for the majority of children to be educated in a public school than to be raised in a public orphanage. We realize, of course, that on Earth you have made a sacred buffalo of the public school."

"Sacred cow," said our Mr. Piper.

"Children and Earthlings should be corrected when they use words wrongly," said Philoxenus. "How else will they learn the correct forms? The animal held sacred in your own near Orient was of the species *Bos bubalus* rather than *Bos bos*, a buffalo rather than a cow. Shall we go to a school?"

"If it cannot be a public school, at least let it be a typical school," said Miss Smice.

"That again is impossible," said Philoxenus. "Every school on Camiroi is, in some respect, atypical."

We went to visit an atypical school.

INCIDENT: Our first contact with the Camiroi students was a violent one. One of them, a lively little boy about eight years old, ran into Miss Munch, knocked her down, and broke her glasses. Then he jabbered something in an unknown tongue.

"Is that Camiroi?" asked Mr. Piper with interest. "From what I have heard, I supposed the language to have a harsher and fuller sound."

"You mean you don't recognize it?" asked Philoxenus with

amusement. "What a droll admission from an educator. The boy is very young and very ignorant. Seeing that you were Earthians, he spoke in Hindi, which is the tongue used by more Earthians than any other. No, no, Xypete, they are of the minority who speak English. You can tell it by their colorless texture and the narrow heads on them."

"I say you sure do have slow reaction, lady," the little boy Xypete explained. "Even subhumans should react faster than that. You just stand there and gape and let me bowl you over. You want me analyze you and see why you react so slow?"

"No! No!"

"You seem unhurt in structure from the fall," the little boy continued, "but if I hurt you I got to fix you. Just strip down to your shift, and I'll go over you and make sure you're all right."

"No! No! No!"

"It's all right," said Philoxenus. "All Camiroi children learn primary medicine in the first grade, setting bones and healing contusions and such."

"No! No! I'm all right. But he's broken my glasses."

"Come along, Earthside lady, I'll make you some others," said the little boy. "With your slow reaction time you sure can't afford the added handicap of defective vision. Shall I fit you with contacts?"

"No. I want glasses just like those which were broken. Oh heavens, what will I do?"

"You come, I do," said the little boy. It was rather revealing to us that the little boy was able to test Miss Munch's eyes, grind lenses, make frames and have her fixed up within three minutes. "I have made some improvements over those you wore before," the boy said, "to help compensate for your slow reaction time."

"Are all the Camiroi students so talented?" Mr. Piper asked. He was impressed.

"No. Xypete is unusual," Philoxenus said. "Most students would not be able to make a pair of glasses so quickly or competently till they were at least nine."

RANDOM INTERVIEWS:

"How rapidly do you read?" Miss Hanks asked a young girl.

"One hundred and twenty words a minute," the girl said.

"On Earth some of the girl students your age have learned to read at the rate of five hundred words a minute," Miss Hanks said proudly.

"When I began disciplined reading, I was reading at the rate of four thousand words a minute," the girl said. "They had quite a time correcting me of it. I had to take remedial reading, and my parents were ashamed of me. Now I've learned to read almost slow enough."

"I don't understand," said Miss Hanks.

"Do you know anything about Earth History or Geography?" Miss Smice asked a middle-sized boy.

"We sure are sketchy on it, lady. There isn't very much over there, is there?"

"Then you have never heard of Dubuque?"

"Count Dubuque interests me. I can't say as much for the city named after him. I always thought that the Count handled the matters of the conflicting French and Spanish land grants and the basic claims of the Sauk and Fox Indians very well. References to the town now carry a humorous connotation, and 'School-Teacher from Dubuque' has become a folk archetype."

"Thank you," said Miss Smice, "or do I thank you?"

"What are you taught of the relative humanity of the Earthians and the Camiroi and of their origins?" Miss Munch asked a Camiroi girl.

"The other four worlds, Earth (Gaea), Kentauron Mikron, Dahae and Astrobe, were all settled from Camiroi. That is what we are taught. We are also given the humorous aside that if it isn't true we will still hold it true till something better comes along. It was we who rediscovered the Four Worlds in historic time, not they who discovered us. If we did not make the original settlements, at least we have filed the first claim that we made them. We did, in historical time, make an additional colonization of Earth. You call it the 'Incursion of the Dorian Greeks.' "

"Where are their playgrounds?" Miss Hanks asked Talarium.

"Oh, the whole world. The children have the run of everything. To set up specific playgrounds would be like setting a table-sized aquarium down in the depths of the ocean. It would really be pointless."

CONFERENCE: The four of us from Earth, specifically from Dubuque, Iowa, were in discussion with the five members of the Camiroi PTA.

"How do you maintain discipline?" Mr. Piper asked.

"Indifferently," said Philoxenus. "Oh, you mean in detail. It varies. Sometimes we let it drift, sometimes we pull them up short. Once they have learned that they must comply to an extent, there is little trouble. Small children are often put down into a pit. They do not eat or come out till they know their assignment."

"But that is inhuman," said Miss Hanks.

"Of course. But small children are not yet entirely human. If a child has not learned to accept discipline by the third or fourth grade, he is hanged."

"Literally?" asked Miss Munch.

"How would you hang a child figuratively? And what effect would that have on the other children?"

"By the neck?" Miss Munch still was not satisfied.

"By the neck until they are dead. The other children always accept the example gracefully and do better. Hanging isn't employed often. Scarcely one child in a hundred is hanged."

"What is this business about slow reading?" Miss Hanks asked. "I don't understand it at all."

"Only the other day there was a child in the third grade who persisted on rapid reading," Philoxenus said. "He was given an object lesson. He was given a book of medium difficulty, and he read it rapidly. Then he had to put the book away and repeat what he had read. Do you know that in the first thirty pages he missed four words? Midway in the book there was a whole statement which he had understood wrongly, and there were hundreds of pages that he got word-perfect only with difficulty. If he was so unsure on material that he had just read, think how imperfectly he would have recalled it forty years later."

"You mean that the Camiroi children learn to recall everything that they read?"

"The Camiroi children and adults will recall for life every detail they have ever seen, read or heard. We on Camiroi are only a little more intelligent than you on Earth. We cannot afford to waste time in forgetting or reviewing, or in pursuing anything of a shallowness that lends itself to scanning."

"Ah, would you call your schools liberal?" Mr. Piper asked.

"I would. You wouldn't," said Philoxenus. "We do not on Camiroi, as you do on Earth, use words to mean their opposites. There is nothing in our education or on our world that corresponds to the quaint servility which you call liberal on Earth."

"Well, would you call your education progressive?"

"No. In your argot, progressive, of course, means infantile."

"How are the schools financed?" asked Mr. Piper.

"Oh, the voluntary tithe on Camiroi takes care of everything, government, religion, education, public works. We don't believe in taxes, of course, and we never maintain a high overhead in anything."

"Just how voluntary is the tithing?" asked Miss Hanks. "Do you sometimes hang those who do not tithe voluntarily?"

"I believe there have been a few cases of that sort," said Philoxenus.

"And is your government really as slipshod as your education?" Mr. Piper asked. "Are your high officials really chosen by lot and for short periods?"

"Oh yes. Can you imagine a person so sick that he would actually *desire* to hold high office for any great period of time? Are there any further questions?"

"There must be hundreds," said Mr. Piper, "but we find difficulty putting them into words."

"If you cannot find words for them, we cannot find answers. PTA disbanded."

CONCLUSIONS: A. The Camiroi system of education is inferior to our own in organization, in buildings, in facilities, in playgrounds, in teacher conferences, in funding, in parental involvement, in supervision, in in-group out-group accommodation adjustment motifs. Some of the school buildings are grotesque. We asked about one particular building which seemed to us to be flamboyant and in bad taste. "What do you expect from second-grade children?" they said. "It is well built even if of peculiar appearance. Second-grade children are not yet complete artists of design."

"You mean that the children designed it themselves?" we asked.

"Of course," they said. "Designed and built it. It isn't a bad job for children."

Such a thing wouldn't be permitted on Earth.

CONCLUSION B. The Camiroi system of education somehow produces much better results than does the education system of Earth. We have been forced to admit this by the evidence at hand.

CONCLUSION C. There is an anomaly as yet unresolved between CONCLUSION A and CONCLUSION B.

We give here, as perhaps of some interest, the curriculum of the Camiroi Primary Education.

FIRST YEAR COURSE:

Playing one wind instrument.

Simple drawing of objects and numbers.

Singing. (This is important. Many Earth people sing who cannot sing. This early instruction of the Camiroi prevents that occurrence.)

Simple arithmetic, hand and machine.

First acrobatics.

First riddles and logic.

Mnemonic religion.

First dancing.

Walking the low wire.

Simple electric circuits.

Raising ants. (Eoempts, not Earth ants.)

SECOND YEAR COURSE:

Playing one keyboard instrument.

Drawing faces, letters, motions.

Singing comedies.

Complex arithmetic, hand and machine.

Second acrobatics.

First jokes and logic.

Quadratic religion.

Second dancing.

Simple defamation. (Spirited attacks on the character of one fellow student, with elementary falsification and simple hatchet-job programming.)

Performing on the medium wire.

Project electric wiring.

Raising bees. (Galelea, not Earth bees.)

THIRD YEAR COURSE:

Playing one stringed instrument.

Reading and voice. (It is here that the student who may have fallen into bad habits of rapid reading is compelled to read at voice speed only.)

Soft stone sculpture.

Situation comedy.

Simple algebra, hand and machine.

First gymnastics.

Second jokes and logic.

Transcendent religion.

Complex acrobatic dancing.

Complex defamation.

Performing on the high wire and the sky pole.

Simple radio construction.

Raising, breeding and dissecting frogs. (Karakoli, not Earth frogs.)

FOURTH YEAR COURSE:

History reading, Camiroi and galactic, basic and geological.

Decadent comedy.

Simple geometry and trigonometry, hand and machine.

Track and field.
Shaggy people jokes and hirsute logic.
Simple obscenity.
Simple mysticism.
Patterns of falsification.
Trapeze work.
Intermediate electronics.
Human dissection.

FIFTH YEAR COURSE:
History reading, Camiroi and galactic, technological.
Introverted drama.
Complex geometries and analytics, hand and machine.
Track and field for fifth form record.
First wit and logic.
First alcoholic appreciation.
Complex mysticism.
Setting intellectual climates, defamation in three dimensions.
Simple oratory.
Complex trapeze work.
Inorganic chemistry.
Advanced electronics.
Advanced human dissection.
Fifth form thesis.

The child is now ten years old, and is half through his primary schooling. He is an unfinished animal, but he has learned to learn.

Sixth Year Course:

Reemphasis on slow reading.

Simple prodigious memory.

History reading, Camiroi and galactic, economic.

Horsemanship (of the Patrushkoe, not the Earth horse).

Advance lathe and machine work for art and utility.

Literature, passive.

Calculi, hand and machine pankration.

Advanced wit and logic.

Second alcoholic appreciation.

Differential religion.

First business ventures.

Complex oratory.

Building scaling. (The buildings are higher and the gravity stronger than on Earth; this climbing of buildings like human flies calls out the ingenuity and daring of the Camiroi children.)

Nuclear physics and post-organic chemistry.

Simple pseudo-human assembly.

Seventh Year Course:

History reading, Camiroi and galactic, cultural.

Advanced prodigious memory.

Vehicle operation and manufacture of simple vehicle.

Literature, active.

Astrognosy, prediction and programming.

Advanced pankration.

Spherical logic, hand and machine.

Advanced alcoholic appreciation.

Integral religion.
Bankruptcy and recovery in business.
Conmanship and trend creation.
Postnuclear physics and universals.
Transcendental athletics endeavor.
Complex robotics and programming.

EIGHTH YEAR COURSE:
History reading, Camiroi and galactic, seminal theory.
Consummate prodigious memory.
Manufacture of complex land and water vehicles.
Literature, compendious and terminative. (Creative book-burning following the Camiroi thesis that nothing ordinary be allowed to survive.)
Cosmic theory, seminal.
Philosophy construction.
Complex hedonism.
Laser religion.
Conmanship, seminal.
Consolidation of simple genius status.
Port-robotic integration.

NINTH YEAR COURSE:
History reading, Camiroi and galactic, future and contingent.
Category invention.
Manufacture of complex light-barrier vehicles.
Construction of simple asteroids and planets.
Matrix religion and logic.
Simple human immortality disciplines.

Consolidation of complex genius status.
First problems of post-consciousness humanity.
First essays in marriage and reproduction.

TENTH YEAR COURSE:

History construction, active.
Manufacture of ultra-light-barrier vehicles.
Panphilosophical clarifications.
Construction of viable planets.
Consolidation of simple sanctity status.
Charismatic humor and pentacosmic logic.
Hypogyroscopic economy.
Penentaglossia. (The perfection of the fifty languages that every educated Camiroi must know including six Earthian languages. Of course the child will already have colloquial mastery of most of these, but he will not yet have them in their full depth.)
Construction of complex societies.
World government. (A course of the same name is sometimes given in Earthian schools, but the course is not of the same content. In this course the Camiroi student will govern a world, though not one of the first aspect worlds, for a period of three or four months.)
Tenth form thesis.

COMMENT ON CURRICULUM:

The child will now be fifteen years old and will have completed his primary education. In many ways he will be advanced beyond his Earth counterpart. Physically more sophisticated, the Camiroi child could kill, with his hands, an Earth-type tiger or a Cape buffalo. An Earth child would perhaps be reluctant even to attempt such feats. The Camiroi boy (or girl) could replace any professional Earth athlete at any position of any game, and could surpass all existing Earth records. It is simply a question of finer poise, strength and speed, the result of adequate schooling.

As to the arts (on which Earthlings sometimes place emphasis) the Camiroi child could produce easy and unequaled masterpieces in any medium. More important, he will have learned the relative unimportance of such pastimes.

The Camiroi child will have failed in business once, at age ten, and have learned patience and perfection of objective by his failure. He will have acquired the techniques of falsification and conmanship. Thereafter he will not be easily deceived by any of the citizens of any of the worlds. The Camiroi child will have become a complex genius and a simple saint; the latter reduces the index of Camiroi crime to near zero. He will be married and settled in those early years of greatest enjoyment.

The child will have built, from materials found around any Camiroi house, a faster-than-light vehicle. He will have piloted it on a significant journey of his own plotting and programming. He will have built quasi-human robots of great intricacy. He will be of perfect memory and judgment and will be well prepared to accept solid learning.

He will have learned to use his whole mind, for the vast reservoirs which are the unconscious to us are not unconscious to him. Everything in him is ordered for use. And there seems to be no great secret about the accomplishments, only to do everything slowly enough and in the right order. Thus they avoid repetition and drill which are the shriveling things which dull the quick apperception.

The Camiroi schedule is challenging to the children, but it is nowhere impossible or discouraging. Everything builds to what follows. For instance, the child is eleven years old before he is given postnuclear physics and universals. Such subjects might be too difficult for him at an earlier age. He is thirteen years old before he undertakes category invention, that intricate course with the simple name. He is fourteen years old when he enters the dangerous field of panphilosophical clarification. But he will have been constructing comprehensive philosophies for two years, and he will have the background for the final clarification.

We should look more closely at this other way of education. In some respects it is better than our own. Few Earth children would be able to construct an organic and sentient robot within fifteen minutes if given the test suddenly; most of them could not manufacture a living dog in that time. Not one Earth child in five could build a faster-than-light vehicle and travel in it beyond our galaxy between now and midnight. Not one Earth child in a hundred could build a planet and have it a going concern within a week. Not one in a thousand would be able to comprehend pentacosmic logic.

RECOMMENDATIONS: A. Kidnapping five Camiroi at random and constituting them a pilot Earth PTA. B. A little constructive book-burning, particularly in the education field. C. Judicious hanging of certain malingering students.

J. F. Bone

Tween

> *Imagine you are a bored adolescent suddenly
> discovering the ability to will what you want.
> Well, what you are imagining is what she did.*

"Leonard," Mr. Ellingsen said, "what on earth are you doing to your hair?"

"Nothing," Lenny said uncomfortably. He glared at Mary Ellen and she looked at him with eyes of greenest innocence. Damned witch, Lenny thought. What Mr. Ellingsen should have said was what in hell is happening to your hair. At least his geography would be more accurate.

"Hmm," Mr. Ellingsen said. "For a moment, it looked as though unseen hands were ruffling it. It was a thoroughly unpleasant sight. I have learned to endure long hair on young men, but I cannot stand watching it rise and fall like waves on a windy beach."

The class laughed and Mary Ellen looked smugly virtuous.

"I didn't do anything," Lenny protested.

"Please don't do it again," Mr. Ellingsen said.

The class giggled and Lenny wished that he was miles away, or that Mary Ellen was—preferably the latter. Just why did she have to pick on him? He wished that he had never dated her last summer. All he'd done was kiss her a couple of times. And he wouldn't have done that if Sue Campbell hadn't been in California with her parents. But the way she'd acted when Sue came back was like they'd been making out ever since Sue left.

It wasn't true. He'd only tried to go further once, and she froze like an icicle. She turned off just like she'd turned a switch. He shrugged. If she wanted to be a cold tomato, that was her bag, but she needn't have acted like she owned him. He dropped her like a hot potato and went back to Sue almost with relief. That was when she started hanging around and being obnoxious. But Sue didn't like Mary Ellen, and that kept the witch away until the end of winter term. Jealousy was strong medicine against witches, Lenny guessed, but it wasn't perfect because Sue and Mary Ellen were talking to each other now.

That wasn't good. Sue was impressionable, and she believed that crap Mary Ellen dished out. Mary Ellen wasn't too truthful when she got going. In fact, she was a goddam liar. But Sue didn't know that. Mary Ellen sure knew how to get Sue worked up.

A guy would be safer with a rattlesnake. At least the snake gave warning before it struck. And its poison was no worse than Mary Ellen's—now she was making cold chills run up and down his spine. They really ran, leaving icy little footprints on his vertebrae. His skin tingled and he shivered uncontrollably.

Mr. Ellingsen looked at him again. A grimace of annoyance twisted the teacher's pallid face.

Lenny began to itch. The urge to scratch was almost uncontrollable.

"Miss Jones," Mr. Ellingsen said.

Mary Ellen shifted her eyes to the teacher. The itching promptly stopped, although the cold spots remained.

"What is there about the back of Leonard's head that demands such intense scrutiny?" Mr. Ellingsen asked.

Mary Ellen blushed.

Lenny felt a mild satisfaction; it served her right. She didn't like being the center of attention. Witches never do. When things began to happen to him a month ago, he'd been suspicious, and after some reading of books in the school and public library he had become certain. He was bewitched. It wasn't something he could talk about, and there wasn't much he could do about it. After all, killing witches was no longer a public service, especially not when they were as pretty as Mary Ellen Jones. Anyway, she was more an annoyance than a danger. She couldn't really harm him now that he was carrying a clove of garlic in his pocket and wore a cross, and a St. Christopher medal. And in three weeks he'd be graduating from dear old John Tyler High and that would be the last of Mary Ellen. He was going to join the Air Force and volunteer for foreign service.

Mary Ellen eyed Mr. Ellingsen with distate. He didn't *have* to call attention to her. He was typical of all that was wrong with male high school teachers, Mary Ellen thought moodily. Possibly he would have turned out better if he had more body and less brains, but slight, balding, nearsighted Mr. Ellingsen, with his high precise voice and quick birdlike movements, was a distinct washout. He was almost as bad as Lenny Stone. She shook her head. No—that wasn't being fair to Mr. Ellingsen. Lenny was unique. Nobody could be as bad—as ugly—as inconsiderate—as horrid as Leonard Joseph Stone. Lord! How she disliked him! It was an emotion that might well develop into a first-class hatred. After all, Mr. Ellingsen was intelligent in a stupid sort of way, which made him different from Lenny. Still, that hardly compensated for his defects. He wasn't human—but then what teacher is? And he was awfully mean to poor Miss Marsden. Everyone knew Anna Marsden was in love with him, but Mr. Ellingsen never gave her a break. He didn't sit with her at the faculty table or walk with her in the hall. He was too wrapped up in Physics to even see a mere English teacher. He was absolutely insufferable. Mary Ellen eyed Ellingsen speculatively. He just might lose some of his offensive superiority if one of his experiments went sour, but nothing ever went wrong with an Ellingsen demonstration. They always went off like clockwork and always proved their point. Mary Ellen sighed. She wished she could do something for Miss Marsden, or do something to Mr. Ellingsen. Either alternative would be more pleasant than just sitting here and listening to things she didn't want to understand. She settled back into a comfortable daydream of experiments going wrong, to the complete frustration of Mr. Ellingsen. . . .

"The object of this demonstration," Mr. Ellingsen said, "is to show that the force of gravity is, to all intents and purposes, a constant when substances of relatively small mass are involved, and that under these conditions, objects will fall at the same velocity regardless of their size and weight. Of course, this is within reasonable limits. I suppose that if you dealt with something as large as the moon, compared with something as small as a steel ball bearing, you would find that the moon would reach the earth sooner because it would attract the earth to it more than the steel ball would, but insofar as the earth's attraction to the moon is concerned, the speeds of attraction would be the same, roughly about 16 feet per second, per second.

"What I'm going to do is show you that a Ping-Pong ball and a steel ball bearing of equal size will fall at the same speed."

"Wouldn't the steel ball hit the ground a lot sooner if you dropped them off a real high place like the top of the clock tower?" Bill Reichart asked. Bill was an honor student and always asked questions. Mr. Ellingsen liked it because it gave him a chance to explain.

"Of course it would, but there are other factors involved."

"Like air resistance?" Lenny asked.

"Exactly. The air would slow the Ping-Pong ball. But if you dropped the two balls through a vacuum they'd fall at the same speed."

"Exactly the same speed?" Reichart persisted.

"Theoretically no—actually yes. The steel ball should attract the earth toward it more than the Ping-Pong ball, but their relative masses are so infinitesimally small as compared with the mass of the earth that the difference is calculable only mathematically and would be expressed in a fractional skil-

116

lionth of a nanosecond. At any rate, there is no instrument in this school that can measure the difference." Mr. Ellingsen was sidestepping the issue. Actually, he wasn't as sure of himself as he had been a few minutes ago. There was something about gravity nibbling at the edges of his memory, but he consoled himself with the thought that if he didn't know, neither did the members of the class. He thought wryly that this was probably why he was teaching high school rather than working for a Nobel price in physics. He simply didn't know enough.

Bill Reichart nodded. "You wouldn't want to bring up Einstein's math?" he asked.

"Not now," Ellingsen said. The class looked relieved. "I'll try to explain," he continued, ignoring the collective subliminal sigh from the students, "but I'll do it with this apparatus. You see, all I want to show at this time is that within practical limits the earth's attraction is a constant. Indeed, it is enough of a constant that Sir Isaac Newton used it as a base for his theory of gravitation and to develop a mathematics that is still useful, despite later discoveries. From a practical viewpoint, we have no need for an analysis of gravity that is more accurate than Newton's, unless we become astronomers or astronauts.

"Now let us examine the demonstration apparatus." Mr. Ellingsen pointed to the two clear plastic tubes behind him that reached from the floor almost to the high ceiling.

"These tubes contain a reasonably hard vacuum," Mr. Ellingsen said. "This will eliminate air resistance. They also contain two dissimilar objects—a Ping-Pong ball and a steel ball bearing, and some electronic apparatus to measure time.

117

The left-hand tube contains the ball bearing and the right-hand tube contains the Ping-Pong ball. The Ping-Pong ball has a few iron filings glued to its surface. Both balls are held in the top of the tubes by electromagnets and there is a sensing device in the bottom of each tube. When I touch this button it will cut the current to the magnets and both balls will be released simultaneously. Now watch what happens. . . ."

Mr. Ellingsen pushed the button.

The Ping-Pong ball smacked against the bottom of the right hand tube but the steel ball remained at the top of its container. With an exclamation of annoyance Mr. Ellingsen punched the button a second time. "Apparently the magnet didn't release," he said uncomfortably. "Well—we'll try again. It's no trouble to reset the balls. All we have to do is turn on the current and invert—" His voice stopped and his eyes bulged. For the steel ball was floating hesitantly down the inside of the tube—moving an inch at a time, pausing occasionally as though to determine whether it was safe to descend another inch. As Mr. Ellingsen peered at the ball, it shivered coyly and retreated to the top of the tube.

"I think I am going mad!" Mr. Ellingsen muttered. "This simply cannot happen. It repeals the Law of Gravity."

Mary Ellen giggled. The sound held a triumphant note.

The whole tube quivered, rose slowly from its metallic base and floated toward the ceiling. Mr. Ellingsen made a frantic grab for the plastic column—and missed.

The class giggled.

Beads of sweat dotted Ellingsen's forehead as he watched the tube snuggle against the ceiling.

"That's a good trick, sir," Bill Reichart said. "How do you do it?"

"I don't," Mr. Ellingsen said unhappily. "It's doing it all by itself."

"I'll bet you do it with wires," Mary Ellen offered helpfully.

"Why should I?" Mr. Ellingsen said in a harassed voice.

"I don't know. Maybe it's a teaching device."

"I intended to teach you about the Law of Gravity—not to repeal it," Mr. Ellingsen replied pettishly. "Both you and I know perfectly well that a thing like this can't happen. It's a physical impossibility. Yet there it is." He gestured hopelessly at the ceiling. "It should be down here."

"But it isn't, sir," Reichart said. "We can all see that. What makes it stay up there?"

"If I knew, do you think I'd be here?" Mr. Ellingsen said. "I'd be so busy patenting the process I wouldn't have time to teach. What you're looking at is antigravity." He looked up at the tube accusingly. "Come down this instant!" he ordered.

The tube dropped on Mr. Ellingsen's head. He went down as though he had been poleaxed—and mixed with the horrified gasp from the class, Lenny could hear Mary Ellen's gloating giggle. . . .

Later, when Mr. Hardesty, the vice-principal, tried to establish the cause of the accident that put Mr. Ellingsen in the hospital with a mild concussion, he came to the conclusion that everyone in Physics 3 was stark, raving mad—including Mr. Ellingsen. The matter was quickly dropped and everyone tried to forget it. Of course, no one did, and it was a six days' wonder until it was replaced with something else. In Home Ec class, about a week later and for no reason at all, plates and glassware sailed across the room and shattered against the wall. Mrs. Albritton, the teacher, was put under the doctor's care, suffering from nervous collapse. Mr. Hardesty told reporters from the school paper that Mrs. Albritton hadn't been feeling well prior to the incident and that everyone hoped she would be better soon. There was no truth in either statement.

The high school baseball team, with worse material than it had the previous year, when it had a 0-10 season, won games with depressing regularity, and by lopsided scores. The ball, no matter who hit it, went for extra bases. And the pitching was uncanny. The only games the team lost were ones a long distance from home, and those losses were by almost as nightmarish scores as the wins near at hand.

"I can't explain it," Mr. Curtis said, as he flexed his Mr. America muscles, "unless we've got a friendly gremlin. I've never coached a team like this. At home we can't do a thing wrong, and on the road we can't do a thing right. If I didn't know better, I'd swear that there's a sorcerer in the stands casting spells for our side. I saw one pitch last night change directions twice. I can't figure it." Curtis's muscles were fine, but his eyes were a bit weak or were playing tricks on him. At least that was what most people figured after listening. And after Mr. Hardesty talked to him it was noticeable that he didn't talk so much about the antics of his baseball team.

Lenny figured it was Mary Ellen's doing. Mr. Curtis was wrong only in the matter of sex. It wasn't a sorcerer. It was a witch. Mary Ellen liked baseball. And she liked to win. Lenny would have bet his last dime that Mary Ellen had hexed the entire baseball team as well as being responsible for everything that went wrong in school . . . and he would have been right.

As Mary Ellen saw it, Anna Marsden was well on her way to becoming an old maid. Even though she was pretty and intelligent, she was twenty-five, which was on the downhill side toward thirty. And everyone knew that thirty was *ancient*! That was mainly because she had to fall in love with that awful stick of a Mr. Ellingsen. Now Mr. Curtis, the baseball coach, was much nicer. Not only did he have hair and muscles, but he had been hanging around the English class for weeks. He said it was because one of his players was having trouble with English Comp, but it was obvious that he liked Miss Marsden. Miss Marsden never gave him a break, which was silly. All she could see was that skinny Mr. Ellingsen—and he never noticed her at all. Miss Marsden would do a lot better with Mr. Curtis. Now if . . .

The scandal erupted two nights later when Mr. Ellingsen broke into Mr. Curtis's apartment and found Miss Marsden. It was only because Mr. Ellingsen was just out of the hospital that Curtis was still alive. Ellingsen had hit him with a bronze table lamp which should have fractured his skull, but due in equal parts to the hardness of Curtis's head and Ellingsen's lack of strength, all the baseball coach suffered was a split scalp. Ellingsen apparently had cause for his actions, since he had been married to Anna Marsden for nearly two months.

"Damned homewrecker!" Mr. Ellingsen snapped from his cell in the city jail. "Casanova! Wife stealer! I hope he's crippled for life. But he won't be," he added gloomily. "I hit the oaf on the head!"

"I never knew she was married, and she never told me," Mr. Curtis explained. "I asked her to come up to my place to look at my Hogarth engravings. She could have refused if she wanted to, but she didn't."

"I don't know what happened. I can't explain it at all," Miss Marsden said wildly. "I love Reggie. I always will. We were going to keep our marriage a secret this year because of this silly school board rule about married couples working in the same school, and earn the down payment on a house. Everything was wonderful until Bill Curtis began chasing after me. I didn't like it and I wanted to tell him so, but I couldn't. I didn't want to go to his apartment, but when he asked me, I said yes. I tried to tell him I was married, but the words wouldn't come. It was like I was sitting outside myself watching something move me like a puppet. It was horrible!"

Sue Campbell ran off with Bill Reichart and got married, and their families were squabbling about an annulment. Bill didn't seem worried about it and Sue had forgotten about becoming a medical missionary and decided to become a mother instead. Somehow she developed an appalling domesticity that made Lenny oddly grateful that things turned out as they did, although for a couple of days he despised Sue and hated Bill. Fortunately it was close enough to graduation that the happy couple were assured of getting their degrees. After that it wouldn't matter. Reichart was going to college and Sue would go with him.

The baseball team won the remainder of its games by lopsided scores, went to the state tournament and was eliminated. Mary Ellen was home in bed with the flu.

Old Mr. Dodds took the wraps off his English History course the last two weeks before finals and gave his students enough details about the Regency Period to arouse a burning love for scatology in the breasts of students who had never cared for history at all. He also gave the class a blanket "A." He was promptly suspended for conduct unbecoming a teacher and went chortling into retirement.

"I've been wanting to do that for thirty years," he chuckled as he made his way through a crowd of admiring students after his last session with the School Board. "For thirty years I've taught emasculated pap for children and I finally got tired of it. This time I gave them the facts."

"What do you intend to do now?" a reporter asked. "The Board can't allow you to continue teaching. They've got you labeled as a menace to society. In Socrates' time they'd have fed you a hemlock cocktail."

"I couldn't care less," Dodds said. "It makes no difference what they do. I'm six months past retirement, so they can't take away my pension. That was my last class. I stayed on only because I was asked." Mr. Dodds chuckled. "I guess I have finally become too old to be worried about anything. I was tired of distorting the truth. Put it down to senile dementia if you wish."

"Your diagnosis may be correct," the reporter said, "but I doubt it."

"You might be right," Dodds replied. "That could have been the only sane act of my entire life."

And while this was going on and the staid order of John Tyler High School was being destroyed, things were happening to Lenny. His shoelaces came untied. His books disappeared. Drinks spilled on him. He stumbled and fell in empty corridors, and suffered embarrassing rips in his trousers. Things were constantly getting in his way. Accidents clung to him as though he was their patron saint. He developed alertness and a sixth sense of impending disaster that enabled him to dodge things like falling fire axes and flower pots. Lenny was certain that Mary Ellen was behind the trouble. He was always conscious of her presence. And gradually, his feeling of resentment and persecution turned from fear to a growing anger. Enough was enough. He had no desire to become a statistic, but he was damned if he'd spend the rest of the school year looking over his shoulder or listening for things that went bump in the dark. He was damned if he was going to duck every time a bird flew over his head. He'd see Mary Ellen alone and settle this once and for all.

It took two days to corner her in a deserted corridor.

"I've taken all I'm going to," Lenny told her fiercely. "Now get off my back and stay off."

"You just think you have, Lenny Stone," Mary Ellen replied. "I haven't even started on you!" Her eyes widened and her slim body tensed. "You're going to regret the day you jilted me!"

"I never—" Lenny began.

"Don't lie! You kissed me last summer, and then went right over to Sue Campbell."

"Good grief—did you think I meant anything? That was

just common courtesy. You girls expect to be kissed. I've known that from junior high."

"No boy ever kissed me before. You lied to me and you'll pay for it."

"The way you're overreacting, a guy would think we made out," Lenny said. "I wouldn't touch you with tongs. You're a weirdo of the worst kind. And if you're worrying about me kissing you—don't. It won't happen again. Just lay off, that's all I ask. I don't want any part of you, anytime. Get out of my life and stay out of it. I don't give a damn what you do to anyone else, even though I know you're responsible for everything that's wrong around here. I don't know how you do it, but so help me, if you try to put the whammy on me again I'll—"

"You'll what?"

"I don't know—but it'll be something drastic."

Mary's body tensed and Lenny felt an overwhelming weight settle on his shoulders. His knees buckled under the strain and his body sagged as it was forced toward the floor. "I'd love to see you crawl!" Mary Ellen gritted. "You snake!"—and he was a snake, complete with skin and scales. He wanted to slither away from here. An empty high school corridor was no place for a snake. He shivered and straightened. This was wrong! He wasn't a snake; he was a man! Sweat poured from his face as he forced his sagging body erect, hands clawing at the air for support. One hand struck Mary Ellen's shoulder, and as it did, a sharp gasp came from the girl. The weight on his back was gone, his scales vanished. Volition rushed back to his muscles—and Mary Ellen writhed on her back on the corridor floor looking up at him with hate-filled eyes. "You pushed me!" she gasped. "You knocked me down!"

"I told you I'd do something if you tried any more fancy tricks," Lenny said heavily. "So long Mary—see you around." He turned from her and walked away, slowly at first. Then he began to run. He skidded around a corner and disappeared.

Mary Ellen rose to her feet. Rage radiated from her. He had made a fool of her again. The window beside her exploded in a burst of flying glass. Two girls coming down the corridor were slammed against the wall. Mary stood in the center of a whirlpool of fury. The floor heaved, a crack appeared in the ceiling, chunks of plaster fell, and a rain of fine gray dust drifted down in crazy patterns through the tortured air.

Mary gasped at the ruin surrounding her. Was *she* doing this? The thought that Lenny might be right crossed her mind, followed by a wave of terror. For if he *was* right, she'd be expelled—maybe even sent to jail! But on the heels of her terror came another thought. If Lenny was right, and she did have this kind of power, there must be a way of controlling it—Mary Ellen's lips curled in a peculiar half smile that was hard and unpleasant. Lenny Stone would whistle a different tune when she got through with him! Meantime, she'd better do something about those two girls. They had seen her and the wreckage that surrounded her, and they would talk. They'd cackle like hens. She'd make them forget—make them forget everything! She began walking slowly toward them. . . .

Emily Jones intruded into her husband's martini with the expertise of nearly two decades of marriage. "John," she said, "this can't go on much longer. Mary Ellen's already damaged the Ellingsens' marriage, got poor Mr. Curtis beat up, put Mrs. Albritton in the hospital, ruined Mr. Dodd's reputation, interfered with the lives of Bill Reichart and Susan Campbell, and made amnesiacs of Ellen Andress and Tami Johnston." Emily eyed her husband accusingly. "You're her father," she said. "Do something! You should have known she'd be a tween before we were done here."

"You're overreacting," Jones said. "Just what can I do? Who can do anything with a tween?"

"We should have watched her more closely. It's our fault."

"For heaven's sake, stop acting like the natives. It's not our fault. Tweens are as old as history. Can't you remember what you were like?"

Emily blushed. "I can," she said, "and that's what worries me."

"Damn it!" Jones said. "It's bad enough living in this crazy breast-beating society without adopting its attributes. I figure we have at least another six months. Kids grow up fast in this environment, but not that fast. We'll be in the Arizona desert working with the Navaho by June and after that phase is over we can go home. I suppose living around sexually mature youngsters fourteen or fifteen years old has some effect but it'll wear off once we get into a more stable environment. However, I'll put your data into the matricizer and run it out."

"What good will that do? What we need is a way to handle Mary Ellen right now. We aren't going to be able to carry this bag of worms by ourselves. You know that."

"We're not going to do a thing as long as they don't suspect her; we're going to keep our hands off. I'm in the final phase of this study and if I abort it now we'll wind up in Limbo, or on the backside of the moon, or some other misbegotten place where we'd be conveniently forgotten. We'd spend the rest of our lives scratching flea bites and shaking dust out of our clothing. We simply have to stick it out."

Emily shook her head. "I think you're wrong, John. There are three weeks left, and by that time—if she keeps growing—Mary Ellen can destroy the school. I don't even want to think of what can happen to the graduation ceremony if she comes to it in as foul a mood as she was in this afternoon. She uprooted a whole row of petunias along the front walk as she came in. Didn't leave a speck of earth on the roots and she never came within three feet of them! I don't think she noticed the damage that followed her from the bus and no one was on the street. No, John, we simply must leave."

"We can't. I can't even pack my records in a week."

"Call a moving company."

"Are you mad? One of those people might be intelligent enough to know what he was packing. Do you want to blow our cover?"

"I want to get out of here."

"Why? No one has accused us of anything. No one suspects Mary Ellen. We can hold out another two or three weeks."

"I suppose you want to wait until she kills someone. Do you want your daughter to be a murderess?"

"She isn't going to kill anyone. She's been raised to respect life."

"And how much does that mean to a tween in the middle of an emotional storm?"

"Damn it, Emily! I'm not going to blow fifteen years' work just to keep an adolescent from acting like an idiot!"

"I wasn't thinking of us—or even of Mary Ellen," Emily said, "I was thinking of the people around us. They're nice inoffensive folks, but they don't really understand what children can do. They take a dim view of vandalism, mayhem, and murder, and they have absolutely no experience handling tweens. If Mary Ellen is discovered as the cause of all this, they might even try to restrain her."

Jones gulped. He had a mental picture of what might happen, and it wasn't pleasant. A chilly grue squiggled down his spine. He shivered and not entirely from the cold. Once the plaster stopped falling and the bodies were removed from the wreckage, his cover would be blown wide open. And naturally, people would draw the wrong conclusions, and a century of study and preparation would go down the drain. The prospect was appalling. "They'd think we were spies," he said. "They might even think we were a prelude to invasion."

"Well—aren't we?"

"Not that way. We want to open trade, not war. We want to exchange technology."

"Doesn't it amount to the same thing in the end? We'll eventually make an economic conquest, and that can be just as bad as a military one."

"No one gets killed."

"Not directly. But the inferior culture doesn't survive. It gets replaced. And in the end we conquer as surely as if we came with bombs and blasters."

John shrugged. "That's not our affair. We have nothing to

do with the economics of empire. We simply collect demographic and sociopolitical data."

"You're being awfully narrow-minded. Can't you remember what happened to Enserala? Or won't you think of what happened to the primitive societies here when they came into contact with Europe? The primitive society always dies except for a few taboos and inconsequential customs."

Jones sighed. He couldn't forget it even though he tried. The path of empire was strewn with the corpses of civilizations and cultures. It was inevitable. One could take some comfort in the thought that nothing could be done to a Class B culture that was half as bad as the things the culture did to itself if it developed in the direction of nation-states. This world had a fairly poor prognosis. Indeed it was a miracle that it has lasted as long as it had. But there was a hard streak of self-preservation in its peoples. At least they'd never started a nuclear war. Somehow despite their mass hysterias, their irrationality, their uncontrolled appetites, their overbreeding, their prides, ideologies, and bigotry, they never took that catastrophic final step. It had aroused Imperial curiosity several decades ago after the first surveys gave the planet a potential lifespan of about fifty standard years. The world had already lasted almost a hundred and seemed in no particular haste to exterminate itself. Yet the inhabitants were to all intents and purposes a nonsurvival type. They were hardly more than tweens without psi—children masquerading as adults. And their continued existence drew the attention of Empire. They might be useful.

"They need to trade with us," Jones said. "We can educate them in the ways of peace and self-control."

"You don't mention that trade is the lifeblood of our society," Emily said. "Without it, we'd have died long ago."

"It gives us a reason for existence," he admitted.

"And increases our power and prestige, and gives our people places to go and things to do."

"It's not our fault that our ancestors overpopulated our world."

"I won't argue that. We're stuck with a demographic fact, and we have learned to live with it, but I don't like thinking that this beautiful world will become another Lyrane."

"Emily—we need this world. The Council has it on first priority. Even though I like these people and don't want to see them hurt, I can't scrap my own loyalties. The survey and investigation *must* go on. Without data we can accomplish nothing."

"They're not going to forgive us if Mary Ellen runs wild," Emily answered.

Jones shrugged. It was a rotten little problem. "Does she hate anyone?" he asked. "Or is she behaving in a reasonably normal tween fashion?"

"I think she doesn't like Lenny Stone, but mainly she's peaking and bottoming out emotionally."

"Is Stone that kid who was hanging around most of last summer? The one whose parents work in the city?"

Emily nodded.

"I can't see why she'd hate him. He's not worth that much thought."

"She's a tween."

"Poor Lenny. I should warn him. It might be well if he left town."

"He'd think you were crazy," Emily said.

"Hey! what's going on here? Are you two plotting something?" Mary Ellen's voice preceded her into the room. "I come down for a glass of milk and find you two whispering over martinis like a pair of spies. What's up?"

Jones looked at his daughter and choked back a reply that sprang to his lips. She was a very satisfactory tween, leggy, elf-faced, with eyes of clearest green that were almost too large. Her bones were good and her body was beginning to mature. Odd that he hadn't noticed—but he'd been busy the last few months. She was tween all right. There was something fey, alien, and appealing about her, like a Keane painting come to life. "It's grown-up talk, sprout," he said. "None of your business."

"We were talking about your future," Emily said.

"Maybe you ought to let me in on it," Mary Ellen said.

"We will, in due time," Emily said blandly. "This talk was about college and money and a career—the kind of background data we have to talk about before we put the savings account on the line."

Such a magnificent liar, John thought with admiration. The diplomatic service lost a star performer when Emily married and went with him on this mission.

"After all, dear, you're our only child and we are concerned about you. The way time passes and the way you kids grow nowadays it's almost no time before you're adults. You'll even be able to vote this fall, and chances are you'll be away from home and in college."

"I don't think I want to go to college."

"Why not?"

"Oh, I don't know. I'm sort of tired of school. It's getting to be a real drag. I think I'd like to get a job, like maybe with the paper, the U.N. or the Peace Corps."

"You're old enough, but you'd be better off in school."

"As usual, you don't understand," Mary Ellen said. "I have to get out. It's—you know—a drag. Irrelevant."

"Stop mouthing," John said. "In the first place I don't know, and in the second there's nothing more relevant to a modern technological society than education."

"You sound like a teacher, Daddy."

"Oh—I won't stop you if you want to get a job. You'll learn a lot from the experience. And besides, if you earn money you can pay board, which will help our budget."

"Mercenary," Mary Ellen said.

Jones grinned. The conversation was safely sidetracked. He hoped that neither the strain nor the relief showed in his face. It had taken a genuine effort to keep from blurting it out when Mary Ellen had wanted a straight answer badly enough to push for it. If it hadn't been for Emily, he might have done just that. He thought bitterly that life had some damnably unpleasant episodes during its passage. This was going to be one of them. There was no question that the girl was dangerous. . . . He'd have to warn Lenny. . . . And he'd have to be prepared to brainwash the kid if he wouldn't listen to reason. . . .

John Jones leaned over the table in the back of McGonigle's Pizza Parlor and looked at the skinny kid with the shock of

133

black hair who sat on the base of his spine and eyed a half-consumed Idiot's Delight pizza and an empty Coke bottle. The boy's face was moody and introspective.

"Are you Lenny Stone?" Jones asked.

"Yeah—that's me."

"I'm Mary Ellen's father."

"I remember you from last summer. And if Mary Ellen's said anything about me, she's lying."

"It's not that. I want to talk with you."

"No way. I don't want anything to do with you—or your daughter. Anything related to Mary Ellen is bad news."

"I don't care what you want. I must warn you. Your life is in danger. Mary Ellen is capable of destroying you. I'm trying to do you a favor."

Lenny shook his head. "Naw—she can't hurt me. All she can do is hurt my friends."

"That's not very charitable."

"Who said I was charitable? Look, Mr. Jones, I hate her guts. She pesters me. She broke up my thing with Sue Campbell. She louses up my classes. The only favor you could do me would be to move far away and take Mary Ellen with you."

"I've considered that," Jones said. He would have been amused if he weren't so worried. Lenny and Emily had the same solution, and the same objections still applied. He couldn't move—not now. It was Lenny who'd have to go. Mary Ellen would murder him! Lenny was a poor innocent idiot playing with the trigger of a loaded machine gun. "The only trouble is that I can't move right now. But maybe you could. I'll pay the expenses."

134

"No way," Lenny said. "No girl is going to run me out of town, and besides, my folks wouldn't let me go." He eyed Jones with a mixture of suspicion and curiosity. He felt drawn to the man. There was none of the strangeness about him that marked his daughter.

"I wish I could do this easily," Jones said, "but I can't. Somehow I have to make you understand that my daughter can kill you, and that she'll probably do just that if you stay around. She has powers most people don't possess."

"You're telling me? She's a witch." Lenny nodded. "I've known that for weeks, but nobody believes me when I tell them. She hexed Mr. Ellingsen. She whammied the baseball team. She—"

"She's not a witch. She's perfectly normal."

"Ha!" Lenny eyed Jones speculatively and wondered if he'd gone too far. Fathers weren't noted for tolerating kids who bad-mouthed their daughters. But, oddly enough, Mr. Jones wasn't affected. He might love Mary Ellen, although Lenny couldn't see why, but the love didn't affect his temper. "Look, sir," Lenny said, "I took Mary Ellen out last summer. I kissed her a few times, but we didn't do anything else, no matter what she says."

"She hasn't said anything except that she hates you. Why did you stop dating?"

"She got too possessive. Acted like she owned me. I didn't like it very much, so I dropped her. A week or so later she chewed me out and told me she hated me."

"When was that?"

"Last September." Lenny shrugged. "She kept telling me

all fall and winter term. Kept saying, 'Just you wait, Lenny Stone. I'll fix you!' "

Jones shivered. "Get out of town, Lenny. I know what I'm talking about. You haven't got a chance."

"But she can't really hurt me. She's tried."

"She hasn't got her full powers yet," Jones said. "The best thing you can do is get away while you still can. Get lost. Vanish. Visit relatives. Don't come back until we're gone. I'm leaving in June—by the tenth I'll be far from here and so will Mary Ellen. You'd be safe then."

"Hey—you're really worried."

"You damn well know I am." Jones stared at Lenny as though he could force his fears and concern into the young man's mind. The light from the window fell on Lenny's face. It had a stark quality not normally found in an adolescent.

Lenny shook his head. "It's my graduation as much as hers," he said. "I belong there as much as she does. I'm staying."

Jones sighed. "All right, Lenny, let's do it the hard way."

"What do you mean by that?"

"This." Jones said. His face hardened and Lenny watched him with mild uneasiness. He was going to get mad after all.

"Are you mad at me for calling Mary Ellen a witch? Are you—hey—leggo—you can't—" Lenny's voice ran down and stopped as he sat with glassy eyes clamped in a fixed stare on Jones's tense face.

This has to be fast, Jones thought. He had perhaps a minute before one of Pop McGonigle's teenage customers was going to notice that Lenny was somewhere on cloud nine. He marshaled what he thought were the most important things for

Lenny's safety, gave the necessary instructions, planted the posthypnotic suggestions, and awakened Lenny.

"Good-bye, Lenny, and good luck," he said.

"Sorry, sir, but I couldn't leave anyway. My parents would object, and I don't have any relatives."

Jones smiled. "Well—you've been warned. I guess that's all I can do. . . ." He walked out of the store feeling reasonably happy. By tomorrow, Lenny should be a hundred miles or more from here. . . .

Mary Ellen faced her father across the dinner table. "What were you talking about with Lenny Stone down at Mc-Gonigle's?" she asked. "And don't say you weren't because I saw you. I want to know."

"Now Mary—" Emily protested.

"*I want to know!*"

"That's no way to talk to your father."

"I don't care—you can't touch me. I've got something that makes me bigger than either of you. I've found out all about it."

"Is the high school still standing?" Jones asked. Sweat broke out on his forehead. He was conscious of a horrid compulsion to tell everything. He clenched his teeth. Mary had at last arrived at control of her powers. She was strong—as strong as Emily had been. He was right when he told Lenny that he couldn't control her—but he hadn't dreamed how right he was. He'd thought he could deny her. That was his worst mistake.

Suddenly he was suspended in midair looking down at the tight angry face of his daughter. The thought that she had learned a lot in a very short time dominated his brain. He had a reasonable certainty that he wasn't going to be hurt physically, even though his position was ridiculous. Adults simply didn't levitate. That was kid stuff.

"Mary! Put your father down this minute!" Emily ordered. She couldn't resist the wry thought that she would love to be in her daughter's place right now. But of course she wasn't, and after all, she couldn't have done a thing like this to John. Still, he *was* a stubborn, opinionated, and unreasonable man at times, and a good shaking would do him a world of good.

"I want to know what he was talking to Lenny about," Mary Ellen said, "and I'm not going to let him down till I do." She smiled a tight, hard, smug little smile. "I've found out what I can do—and how to do it," she said. "I'm maybe the most powerful person in the world. And you're going to tell me what I want to know and do what I want you to do—or—I'll—"

"You'll what?" Lenny asked. He stood in the kitchen door, looking at the suddenly frozen tableau. There was a solid thump as Jones's buttocks made contact with the floor, followed by three lesser thumps as heels and head followed the example of his behind. He scrambled to his feet, his face a study in anger and embarrassment.

"You!" Mary Ellen screeched at Lenny. "Go away! Get out of here!"

"Why?"

"Thanks," Jones said. "I'm glad you showed up, but you should be running for your life."

"Mom said you did a pretty good job for a quickie," Lenny

said. "You left only a couple of loose ends. But those were enough. You gave me no motivation that would stand probing. I don't know that I told you, but I can't hide anything from Mom. Anyway, it looks as though I came just in time."

"You did. I'm too old to appreciate being the centrum of a psi effect."

"I told you to get out of here," Mary Ellen said, glaring at Lenny.

"Get lost," Lenny said.

Jones shuddered. In about ten seconds there would be bloodshed.

"I am going to wring you out and hang you up to dry," Mary Ellen said. "I am going to smash you and shred the pieces. I am going to break you into little bits. I know what I can do!"

"Big talk," Lenny said. He stood in front of her, his face twisted into a mocking grin. "There's a lot of hot air in you that ought to be let out," he said. "You're all puffed up. Your hubris is showing. You need deflating."

Mary Ellen ground her teeth and her face turned livid with anger.

"Run!" Emily gasped. "You've gone too far! She'll kill you!"

The air in the room thickened and writhed and became a gelid something that wasn't air. Forces gathered, poised, pulsed, and as Mary Ellen paused to focus the effect, Lenny reached out and touched her. Something snatched Mary Ellen, spun her through the air and bounced her off the floor! The room shook, the walls creaked, plaster fell, and a dead calm descended upon the Jones kitchen.

Emily's eyes opened with a mixture of amazement and

realization. Jones grinned, and Mary Ellen looked at Lenny with hate-filled eyes. "You did it again!" she said. "Damn you!"

"It's a good thing you have a well-padded behind," Lenny said. "That was quite a wallop."

"It hurts," Mary Ellen said.

"Maybe it'll teach you not to act stupid," Lenny said. "I told your dad that you couldn't hurt me. You can't. You and I—we're complements. We cancel out. You're a psi positive. I'm negative. It's a defense mechanism our race has had from the beginning. We'd never have survived if a bunch of nutty tweens could damage each other and everyone else because they had no self-control. Of course psi effects were useful to discourage predators and other big terrifying things. But except for telepathy they're no good to help the race become civilized. When you can't lie you've gotta be honest. But psychokinetics such as you have are no good for anything nowadays."

"What are you talking about? I don't get it."

"Don't worry, you will as soon as your mom gets through talking to you. My Mom told me about it before she sent me over here. And I guess it's a good thing she did. You were making an idiot out of yourself and you might have done something real bad. You can't help being a tween any more than I can—it's part of growing up. But you can help being stupid."

Mary Ellen got slowly to her feet. It dawned on her that she was abysmally ignorant, and from the expressions on her parents' faces she realized that she was the only one who was. Her parents knew exactly what Lenny was saying. It wasn't fair, she thought. And from the relaxed smile on her father's face she was certain that whatever had happened, it was something that took a monkey off his back. The thought was ambivalent.

"Just keep a hand on her, Lenny," Jones said. "Emily's bound to have her bracelets around somewhere. She never throws anything away." Jones sighed with relief. "I suppose I should have guessed. You practically told me down at McGonigle's, but I wasn't thinking very well. I had a mental picture of you on a marble slab."

"Don't worry about the bracelets," Lenny said. "Mom gave me hers. She figured you might need them." He reached into his jacket pocket and took out a plain gold bracelet. There wasn't anything unusual about it except that it locked with a final-sounding click when he closed it around Mary Ellen's wrist. "I'm wearing the mate to it," Lenny said, pushing back the left sleeve of his jacket to show an identical bracelet around his lean wrist. "She can't do anything now. As long as I'm around, she's neutralized."

"It's a miracle!" Emily said. "To think that there was a complementary—why the odds against it are in the millions!"

"Not quite," Lenny said. "You see, Mrs. Jones, my folks were transferred from Chicago because my psych profile and Mary Ellen's were almost identical. The—the Council?"— he paused and Jones nodded. "The Council," Lenny continued, "thought Mary Ellen would go tween earlier on this world than on Lyrane—something to do with the kind of sunlight and the shortness of the years. Since my pattern fitted hers to four decimal points, they figured I was almost certainly complementary, so they sent my parents here. I guess you have a higher research priority than Dad. Anyway, I don't know much about these things."

"I expect we should have told Mary Ellen," Emily said.

"You should have," Lenny said. "Tweens aren't really stupid or uncooperative, we're merely young."

"Have you learned the standing rules?" Jones asked.

"No, but Mom said that was why we never got in touch. We were ready if needed, but we weren't supposed to contact you. That was why she broke me off with Mary Ellen last summer. I kinda liked her, but Mom brainwashed it out of me. It might have been better if she hadn't. Besides, she thinks you're crazy to bring a girl here."

"Mary Ellen was born here," Emily said.

"You're going to stay with us, of course," Jones said.

"Naturally. Your assignment's about over and Mom wants me to go home for advanced training. I think I'd like to be a psychologician, and you can't get that sort of education on this world. My folks say it's all right if I go with you to Arizona. They'll both be interested in financial operations this summer. And when you're done I can go home with you."

"Good!" Emily said.

Mary Ellen shook her head. "I won't stand for this," she said. "If Lenny comes into this house, I'm leaving!"

"You're not going anywhere," Lenny said, "or doing anything except graduate from dear old John Tyler High. After that, you and I and your parents are going to take a long trip to a place called Lyrane. And when the people there get through with us, we'll be adults. And maybe then I won't look so much like a louse to you, and you won't look so much like a witch to me."

"Mom!—*do* something!"

Emily shrugged. Her pleasant face wore a tight Gioconda smile, half loving, half cruel. Looking at her, Jones wondered if the Mona Lisa had been a Lyranian. It was hardly possible, but there was more than a passing resemblance. "Dear," Emily said, "I can't do a thing about it. You'll simply have to grow up and become decently inhuman."

Edward D. Hoch

Zoo

*Do we have bars in a zoo to protect us from
the animals, or is there another reason?*

The children were always good during the month of August,
especially when it began to get near the twenty-third. It was
on this day that the great silver spaceship carrying Professor
Hugo's Interplanetary Zoo settled down for its annual six-hour
visit to the Chicago area.

Before daybreak the crowds would form, long lines of children and adults both, each one clutching his or her dollar,
and waiting with wonderment to see what race of strange creatures the Professor had brought this year.

In the past they had sometimes been treated to three-legged
creatures from Venus, or tall, thin men from Mars, or even
snakelike horrors from somewhere more distant. This year, as
the great round ship settled slowly to earth in the huge tri-city
parking area just outside of Chicago, they watched with awe
as the sides slowly slid up to reveal the familiar barred cages.

In them were some wild breed of nightmare—small, horselike animals that moved with quick, jerking motions and constantly chattered in a high-pitched tongue. The citizens of Earth clustered around as Professor Hugo's crew quickly collected the waiting dollars, and soon the good Professor himself made an appearance, wearing his many-colored rainbow cape and top hat. "Peoples of Earth," he called into his microphone.

The crowd's noise died down and he continued. "Peoples of Earth, this year you see a real treat for your single dollar— the little-known horse-spider people of Kaan—brought to you across a million miles of space at great expense. Gather around, see them, study them, listen to them, tell your friends about them. But hurry! My ship can remain here only six hours!"

And the crowds slowly filed by, at once horrified and fascinated by these strange creatures that looked like horses but ran up the walls of their cages like spiders. "This is certainly worth a dollar," one man remarked, hurrying away. "I'm going home to get the wife."

All day long it went like that, until ten thousand people had filed by the barred cages set into the side of the spaceship. Then, as the six-hour limit ran out, Professor Hugo once more took microphone in hand. "We must go now, but we will return next year on this date. And if you enjoyed our zoo this year, phone your friends in other cities about it. We will land in New York tomorrow, and next week on to London, Paris, Rome, Hong Kong, and Tokyo. Then on to other worlds!"

He waved farewell to them, and as the ship rose from the ground the Earth peoples agreed that this had been the very best Zoo yet. . . .

Some two months and three planets later, the silver ship of Professor Hugo settled at last onto the familiar jagged rocks of Kaan, and the queer horse-spider creatures filed quickly out of their cages. Professor Hugo was there to say a few parting words, and then they scurried away in a hundred different directions, seeking their homes among the rocks.

In one, the she-creature was happy to see the return of her mate and offspring. She babbled a greeting in the strange tongue and hurried to embrace them. "It was a long time you were gone. Was it good?"

And the he-creature nodded. "The little one enjoyed it especially. We visited eight worlds and saw many things."

The little one ran up the wall of the cave. "On the place called Earth it was the best. The creatures there wear garments over their skins, and they walk on two legs."

"But isn't it dangerous?" asked the she-creature.

"No," her mate answered. "There are bars to protect us from them. We remain right in the ship. Next time you must come with us. It is well worth the nineteen commocs it costs."

And the little one nodded. "It was the very best Zoo ever. . . ."

Zenna Henderson

Subcommittee

> *What will peace negotiations with aliens be like?*
> *They could be dangerous, or as easy*
> *as child's play.*

First came the sleek black ships, falling out of the sky in patterned disorder, sowing fear as they settled like seeds on the broad landing field. After them, like bright butterflies, came the vividly colored slow ships that hovered and hesitated and came to rest scattered among the deadly dark ones.

"Beautiful!" sighed Serena, turning from the conference room window. "There should have been music to go with it."

"A funeral dirge," said Thorn. "Or a requiem. Or flutes before failure. Frankly, I'm frightened, Rena. If these conferences fail, all hell will break loose again. Imagine living another year like this past one."

"But the conference won't fail!" Serena protested. "If they're willing to consent to the conference, surely they'll be willing to work with us for peace."

"Their peace or ours?" asked Thorn, staring morosely out

the window. "I'm afraid we're being entirely too naïve about this whole affair. It's been a long time since we finally were able to say, 'Ain't gonna study war no more,' and made it stick. We've lost a lot of the cunning that used to be necessary in dealing with other people. We can't, even now, be sure this isn't a trick to get all our high command together in one place for a grand massacre."

"Oh, no!" Serena pressed close to him and his arm went around her. "They couldn't possibly violate—"

"Couldn't they?" Thorn pressed his cheek to the top of her ear. "We don't know, Rena. We just don't know. We have so little information about them. We know practically nothing about their customs—even less about their values, or from what frame of reference they look upon our suggestion of suspending hostilities."

"But surely they must be sincere. They brought their families along with them. You did say those bright ships are family craft, didn't you?"

"Yes, they suggested we bring our families and they brought their families along with them, but it's nothing to give us comfort. They take them everywhere—even into battle."

"Into battle!"

"Yes. They mass the home craft off out of range during battles, but every time we disable or blast one of their fighters, one or more of the home craft spin away out of control or flare into nothingness. Apparently they're just glorified trailers, dependent on the fighters for motive power and everything else." The unhappy lines deepened in Thorn's face. "They don't know it, but even apart from their superior weapons, they practically forced us into this truce. How could we go on wiping out their war fleet when, with every black ship, those confounded posy-colored home craft fell too, like pulling petals off a flower. And each petal heavy with the lives of women and children."

Serena shivered and pressed closer to Thorn. "The conference must work. We just can't have war anymore. You've got to get through to them. Surely, if we want peace and so do they—"

"We don't know what they want," said Thorn heavily. "Invaders, aggressors, strangers from hostile worlds—so completely alien to us—how can we ever hope to get together?"

They left the conference room in silence, snapping the button on the doorknob before they closed it.

"Hey, lookit, Mommie! Here's a wall!" Splinter's five-year-old hands flattened themselves like grubby starfish against the greenish ripple of the ten-foot vitricrete fence that wound through the trees and slid down the gentle curve of the hill. "Where did it come from? What's it for? How come we can't go play in the go'fish pond anymore?"

Serena leaned her hand against the wall. "The people who came in the pretty ships wanted a place to walk and play, too. So the Construction Corp put the fence up for them."

"Why won't they let me play in the go'fish pond?" Splinter's brows bent ominously.

"They don't know you want to," said Serena.

"I'll tell them, then," said Splinter. He threw his head back. "Hey! Over there!" he yelled, his fists doubling and his whole

149

body stiffening with the intensity of the shout. "Hey! I wanta play in the go'fish pond!"

Serena laughed. "Hush, Splinter. Even if they could hear you, they wouldn't understand. They're from far, far away. They don't talk the way we do."

"But maybe we could play," said Splinter wistfully.

"Yes," sighed Serena, "maybe you could play. If the fence weren't there. But you see, Splinter, we don't know what kind of—people—they are. Whether they would want to play. Whether they would be—nice."

"Well, how can we find out with that old wall there?"

"We can't, Splinter," said Serena. "Not with the fence there."

They walked on down the hill, Splinter's hand trailing along the wall.

"Maybe they're mean," he said finally. "Maybe they're so bad that the 'struction Corp had to build a cage for them—a big, big cage!" He stretched his arm as high as he could reach, up the wall. "Do you suppose they got tails?"

"Tails?" laughed Serena. "Whatever gave you that idea?"

"I dunno. They came from a long ways away. I'd like a tail—a long, curly one with fur on!" He swished his miniature behind energetically.

"Whatever for?" asked Serena.

"It'd come in handy," said Splinter solemnly. "For climbing and—and keeping my neck warm!"

"Why aren't there any other kids here?" he asked as they reached the bottom of the slope. "I'd like *somebody* to play with."

"Well, Splinter, it's kind of hard to explain," started Serena, sinking down on the narrow ledge shelving on the tiny dry watercourse at her feet.

"Don't esplain then," said Splinter. "Just tell me."

"Well, some Linjeni generals came in the big black ships to talk with General Worsham and some more of our generals. They brought their families with them in the fat, pretty ships. So our generals brought their families, too, but your daddy is the only one of our generals who has a little child. All the others are grown up. That's why there's no one for you to play with." I wish it were as simple as it sounds, thought Serena, suddenly weary again with the weeks of negotiation and waiting that had passed.

"Oh," said Splinter, thoughtfully. "Then there *are* kids on the other side of the wall, aren't there?"

"Yes, there must be young Linjeni," said Serena. "I guess you could call them children."

Splinter slid down to the bottom of the little watercourse and flopped down on his stomach. He pressed his cheek to the sand and peered through a tiny gap left under the fence where it crossed the stream bed. "I can't see anybody," he said, disappointed.

They started back up the hill toward their quarters, walking silently, Splinter's hand whispering along the wall.

"Mommie?" Splinter said as they neared the patio.

"Yes, Splinter?"

"That fence is to keep them in, isn't it?"

"Yes," said Serena.

"It doesn't feel like that to me," said Splinter. "It feels like it's to shut me out."

Serena suffered through the next days with Thorn. She lay wide-eyed beside him in the darkness of their bedroom, praying as he slept restlessly, struggling even in his sleep—groping for a way.

Tight-lipped, she cleared away untouched meals and brewed more coffee. Her thoughts went hopefully with him every time he started out with new hope and resolution, and her spirits flagged and fell as he brought back dead end, stalemate and growing despair. And in between times, she tried to keep Splinter on as even a keel as possible, giving him the freedom of the Quarters Area during the long, sunlit days and playing with him as much as possible in the evenings.

One evening Serena was pinning up her hair and keeping half an eye on Splinter as he splashed in his bath. He was gathering up handfuls of foaming soap bubbles and pressing them to his chin and cheeks.

"Now I hafta shave like Daddy," he hummed to himself. "Shave, shave, shave!" He flicked the suds off with his forefinger. Then he scooped up a big double handful of bubbles and pressed them all over his face. "Now I'm Doovie. I'm all over fuzzy like Doovie. Lookit, Mommie, I'm all over—" He opened his eyes and peered through the suds to see if she was watching. Consequently, Serena spent a busy next few minutes helping him get the soap out of his eyes. When the tears had finally washed away the trouble, Serena sat toweling Splinter's relaxed little body.

"I bet Doovie'd cry too, if he got soap in his eyes," he said with a sniff. "Wouldn't he, Mommie?"

"Doovie?" said Serena, "Probably. Almost anyone would. Who's Doovie?"

She felt Splinter stiffen on her lap. His eyes wandered away from hers. "Mommie, do you think Daddy will play with me a-morrow?"

"Perhaps." She captured one of his wet feet. "Who's Doovie?"

"Can we have pink cake for dessert tonight? I think I like pink—"

"Who's Doovie?" Serena's voice was firm. Splinter examined his thumbnail critically, then peered up at Serena out of the corner of his eye.

"Doovie," he began, "Doovie's a little boy."

"Oh?" said Serena. "A playlike little boy?"

"No," Splinter whispered, hanging his head. "A real little boy. A Linjeni little boy." Serena drew an astonished breath and Splinter hurried on, his eyes intent on hers. "He's nice people, Mommie, honest! He doesn't say bad words or tell lies or talk sassy to his mother. He can run as fast as I can— faster, if I stumble. He—he—" His eyes dropped again. "I like him—" His mouth quivered.

"Where did—how could—I mean, the fence—" Serena was horrified and completely at a loss for words.

"I dug a hole," confessed Splinter. "Under the fence where the sand is. You didn't say not to! Doovie came to play. His mommie came, too. She's pretty. Her fur is pink, but Doovie's is nice and green. All over!" Spinter got excited. "All over, even where his clothes are! All but his nose and eyes and ears and the front of his hands!"

"But Splinter, how could you! You might have got hurt!

153

They might have—" Serena hugged him tight to hide her face from him.

Splinter squirmed out of her arms. "Doovie wouldn't hurt anyone. You know what, Mommie? He can shut his nose! Yes, he can! He can shut his nose and fold up his ears! I wish I could. It'd come in handy. But I'm bigger'n he is and I can sing and he can't. But he can whistle with his nose and when I try, I just blow mine. Doovie's nice!"

Serena's mind was churning as she helped Splinter get into his night clothes. She felt the chill of fear along her forearms and the back of her neck. What to do now? Forbid Splinter's crawling under the fence? Keep him from possible danger that might just be biding its time? What would Thorn say? Should she tell him? This might precipitate an incident that—

"Splinter, how many times have you played with Doovie?"

"How many?" Splinter's chest swelled under his clean pajamas. "Let me count," he said importantly and murmured and mumbled over his fingers for a minute. "Four times!" he proclaimed triumphantly. "One, two, three, four whole times!"

"Weren't you scared?"

"Naw!" he said, adding hastily, "Well, maybe a little bit the first time. I thought maybe they might have tails that liked to curl around people's necks. But they haven't," disappointed, "only clothes on like us with fur on under."

"Did you say you saw Doovie's mother, too?"

"Sure," said Splinter. "She was there the first day. She was the one that sent all the others away when they all crowded around me. All grownups. Not any kids excepting Doovie. They kinda pushed and wanted to touch me, but she told them to go away, and they all did 'cepting her and Doovie."

"Oh, Splinter!" cried Serena, overcome by the vision of his small self surrounded by pushing, crowding Linjeni grown-ups who wanted to "touch" him.

"What's the matter, Mommie?" asked Splinter.

"Nothing, dear." She wet her lips. "May I go along with you the next time you go to see Doovie? I'd like to meet his mother."

"Sure, sure!" cried Splinter. "Let's go now. Let's go now!"

"Not now," said Serena, feeling the reaction of her fear in her knees and ankles. "It's too late. Tomorrow we'll go see them. And Splinter, let's not tell Daddy yet. Let's keep it a surprise for a while."

"Okay, Mommie," said Splinter. "It's a good surprise, isn't it? You were awful surprised, weren't you?"

"Yes, I was," said Serena. "Awful surprised."

Next day Splinter squatted down and inspected the hole under the fence. "It's kinda little," he said. "Maybe you'll get stuck."

Serena, her heart pounding in her throat, laughed. "That wouldn't be very dignified, would it?" she asked. "To go calling and get stuck in the door."

Splinter laughed. "It'd be funny," he said. "Maybe we better go find a really door for you."

"Oh, no," said Serena hastily. "We can make this one bigger."

"Sure," said Splinter. "I'll go get Doovie and he can help dig."

"Fine," said Serena, her throat tightening. *Afraid of a child*, she mocked herself. *Afraid of a Linjeni—aggressor—invader*, she defended.

Splinter flattened on the sand and slid under the fence. "You start digging," he called. "I'll be back!"

Serena knelt to the job, the loose sand coming away so readily that she circled her arms and dredged with them.

Then she heard Splinter scream.

For a brief second, she was paralyzed. Then he screamed again, closer, and Serena dragged the sand away in a frantic frenzy. She felt the sand scoop down the neck of her blouse and the skin scrape off her spine as she forced herself under the fence.

Then there was Splinter, catapulting out of the shrubbery, sobbing and screaming, "Doovie! Doovie's drownding! He's in the go'fish pond! All under the water! I can't get him out! Mommie, Mommie!"

Serena grabbed his hand as she shot past and towed him along, stumbling and dragging, as she ran for the goldfish pond. She leaned across the low wall and caught a glimpse, under the churning thrash of the water, of green mossy fur and staring eyes. With hardly a pause except to shove Splinter backward and start a deep breath, she plunged over into the pond. She felt the burning bite of water up her nostrils and grappled in the murky darkness for Doovie—feeling again and again the thrash of small limbs that slipped away before she could grasp them.

Then she was choking and sputtering on the edge of the pond, pushing the still struggling Doovie up and over. Splinter grabbed him and pulled as Serena heaved herself over the edge of the pond and fell sprawling across Doovie.

Then she heard another higher, shriller scream and was

shoved off Doovie viciously, and Doovie was snatched up into rose-pink arms. Serena pushed her lank, dripping hair out of her eyes and met the hostile glare of the rose-pink eyes of Doovie's mother.

Serena edged over to Splinter and held him close, her eyes intent on the Linjeni. The pink mother felt the green child all over anxiously, and Serena noticed with an odd detachment that Splinter hadn't mentioned that Doovie's eyes matched his fur and that he had webbed feet.

Webbed feet! She began to laugh, almost hysterically. Oh Lordy! No wonder Doovie's mother was so alarmed.

"Can you talk to Doovie?" asked Serena of the sobbing Splinter.

"No!" wailed Splinter. "You don't have to talk to play."

"Stop crying, Splinter," said Serena. "Help me think. Doovie's mother thinks we were trying to hurt Doovie. He wouldn't drown in the water. Remember, he can close his nose and fold up his ears. How are we going to tell his mother we weren't trying to hurt him?"

"Well," Splinter scrubbed his cheeks with the back of his hand. "We could hug him—"

"That wouldn't do, Splinter," said Serena, noticing with near panic that the other brightly colored figures were moving among the shrubs, drawing closer— "I'm afraid she won't let us touch him."

Briefly she toyed with the idea of turning and trying to get back to the fence; then she took a deep breath and tried to calm down.

"Let's play-like, Splinter," she said. "Let's show Doovie's

mother that we thought he was drowning. You go fall in the pond and I'll pull you out. You play-like drowned and I'll— I'll cry."

"Gee, Mommie, you're crying already!" said Splinter, his face puckering.

"I'm just practicing," she said, steadying her voice. "Go on."

Splinter hesitated on the edge of the pond, shrinking away from the water that had fascinated him so many times before. Serena screamed suddenly, and Splinter, startled, lost his balance and fell in. Serena had hold of him almost before he went underwater and pulled him out, cramming as much of fear and apprehension into her voice and actions as she could. "Be dead," she whispered fiercely. "Be dead all over!" And Splinter melted so completely in her arms that her moans and cries of sorrow were only partly make-believe. She bent over his still form and rocked to and fro in her grief.

A hand touched her arm and she looked up into the bright eyes of the Linjeni. The look held for a long moment and then the Linjeni smiled, showing even, white teeth, and a pink, furry hand patted Splinter on the shoulder. His eyes flew open and he sat up. Doovie peered around from behind his mother and then he and Splinter were rolling and tumbling together, wrestling happily between the two hesitant mothers. Serena found a shaky laugh somewhere in among her alarms and Doovie's mother whistled softly with her nose.

That night, Thorn cried out in his sleep and woke Serena. She lay in the darkness, her constant prayer moving like a candle flame in her mind. She crept out of bed and checked Splinter in his shadowy room. Then she knelt and opened the bottom drawer of Splinter's chest-robe. She ran her hand over the gleaming folds of the length of Linjeni material that lay there—the material the Linjeni had found to wrap her in while her clothes dried. She had given them her lacy slip in exchange. Her fingers read the raised pattern in the dark, remembering how beautiful it was in the afternoon sun. Then the sun was gone and she saw a black ship destroyed, a home craft plunging to incandescent death, and the pink and green and yellow and all the other bright furs charring and crisping, and the patterned materials curling before the last flare of flame. She leaned her head on her hand and shuddered.

But then she saw the glitter of a silver ship, blackening and fusing, dripping monstrously against the emptiness of space. And heard the wail of a fatherless Splinter so vividly that she shoved the drawer in hastily and went back to look at his quiet, sleeping face, and to tuck him unnecessarily in.

When she came back to bed, Thorn was awake, lying on his back, his elbows winging out.

"Awake?" she asked as she sat down on the edge of the bed.

"Yes." His voice was tense as the twang of a wire. "We're getting nowhere," he said. "Both sides keep holding up neat little hoops of ideas, but no one is jumping through, either way. We want peace, but we can't seem to convey anything to them. They want something, but they haven't said what, as though to tell us would betray them irrevocably into our hands, but they won't make peace unless they can get it. Where do we go from here?"

"If they'd just go away—" Rena swung her feet up onto the bed and clasped her slender ankles with both hands.

"That's one thing we've established." Thorn's voice was bitter, "They *won't* go. They're here to stay—like it or not."

"Thorn—" Rena spoke impulsively into the shadowy silence. "Why don't we just make them welcome? Why can't we just say, 'Come on in!' They're travelers from afar. Can't we be hospitable—"

"You talk as though the afar was just the next county—or state!" Thorn tossed impatiently on the pillow.

"Don't tell me we're back to that old equation—Stranger equals Enemy," said Rena, her voice sharp with strain. "Can't we assume they're friendly? Go visit with them—talk with them casually—"

"Friendly!" Thorn shot upright from the tangled bedclothes. "Go visit! Talk!" His voice choked off. Then carefully, calmly he went on. "Would you care to visit with the widows of our men who went to visit the friendly Linjeni? Whose ships dropped out of the sky without warning—"

"Theirs did, too." Rena's voice was small but stubborn. "With no more warning than we had. Who shot first? You must admit no one knows for sure."

There was a tense silence; then Thorn lay down slowly, turned his back to Serena and spoke no more.

"Now I can't ever tell," mourned Serena into her crumpled pillow. "He'd die if he knew about the hole under the fence."

In the days that followed, Serena went every afternoon with Splinter and the hole under the fence got larger and larger.

Doovie's mother, whom Splinter called Mrs. Pink, was teaching Serena to embroider the rich materials like the length they had given her. In exchange, Serena was teaching Mrs. Pink how to knit. At least, she started to teach her. She got as far as purl and knit, decrease and increase, when Mrs. Pink took the work from her, and Serena sat widemouthed at the incredible speed and accuracy of Mrs. Pink's furry fingers. She felt a little silly for having assumed that the Linjeni didn't know about knitting. And yet, the other Linjeni crowded around and felt of the knitting and exclaimed over it in their soft, fluty voices as though they'd never seen any before. The little ball of wool Serena had brought was soon used up, but Mrs. Pink brought out hanks of heavy thread such as were split and used in their embroidery, and after a glance through Serena's pattern book, settled down to knitting the shining brilliance of Linjeni thread.

Before long, smiles and gestures, laughter and whistling, were not enough. Serena sought out the available tapes—a scant handful—on Linjeni speech and learned them. They didn't help much since the vocabulary wasn't easily applied to the matters she wanted to discuss with Mrs. Pink and the others. But the day she voiced and whistled her first Linjeni sentence to Mrs. Pink, Mrs. Pink stumbled through her first English sentence. They laughed and whistled together and settled down to pointing and naming and guessing across areas of incommunication.

Serena felt guilty by the end of the week. She and Splinter were having so much fun and Thorn was wearier and wearier at each session's end.

161

"They're impossible," he said bitterly, one night, crouched forward tensely on the edge of his easy chair. "We can't pin them down to anything."

"What do they want?" asked Serena. "Haven't they said yet?"

"I shouldn't talk—" Thorn sank back in his chair. "Oh, what does it matter?" he asked wearily. "It'll all come to nothing anyway!"

"Oh, no, Thorn!" cried Serena. "They're reasonable human—" she broke off at Thorn's surprised look. "Aren't they?" she stammered. "Aren't they?"

"Human? They're uncommunicative, hostile aliens," he said. "We talk ourselves blue in the face and they whistle at one another and say yes or no. Just that, flatly."

"Do they understand—" began Serena.

"We have interpreters, such as they are. None too good, but all we have."

"Well, what are they asking?" asked Serena.

Thorn laughed shortly. "So far as we've been able to ascertain, they just want all our oceans and the land contiguous thereto."

"Oh, Thorn, they couldn't be that unreasonable!"

"Well I'll admit we aren't even sure that's what they mean, but they keep coming back to the subject of the oceans, except they whistle rejection when we ask them point-blank if it's the oceans they want. There's just no communication." Thorn sighed heavily. "You don't know them like we do, Rena."

"No," said Serena, miserably. "Not like you do."

She took her disquiet, Splinter, and a picnic basket down

the hill to the hole next day. Mrs. Pink had shared her lunch with them the day before, and now it was Serena's turn. They sat on the grass together, Serena crowding back her unhappiness to laugh at Mrs. Pink and her first olive with the same friendly amusement Mrs. Pink had shown when Serena had bit down on her first *pirwit* and had been afraid to swallow it and ashamed to spit it out.

Splinter and Doovie were agreeing over a thick meringued lemon pie that was supposed to be dessert.

"Leave the pie alone, Splinter," said Serena. "It's to top off on."

"We're only tasting the fluffy stuff," said Splinter, a blob of meringue on his upper lip bobbing as he spoke.

"Well, save your testing for later. Why don't you get out the eggs. I'll bet Doovie isn't familiar with them either."

Splinter rummaged in the basket, and Serena took out the huge camp salt shaker.

"Here they are, Mommie!" cried Splinter. "Lookit, Doovie, first you have to crack the shell—"

Serena began initiating Mrs. Pink into the mysteries of hardboiled eggs and it was all very casual and matter of fact until she sprinkled the peeled egg with salt. Mrs. Pink held out her cupped hand and Serena sprinkled a little salt into it. Mrs. Pink tasted it.

She gave a low whistle of astonishment and tasted again. Then she reached tentatively for the shaker. Serena gave it to her, amused. Mrs. Pink shook more into her hand and peered through the holes in the cap of the shaker. Serena unscrewed the top and showed Mrs. Pink the salt inside it.

For a long minute Mrs. Pink stared at the white granules and then she whistled urgently, piercingly. Serena shrank back, bewildered, as every bush seemed to erupt Linjeni. They crowded around Mrs. Pink, staring into the shaker, jostling one another, whistling softly. One scurried away and brought back a tall jug of water. Mrs. Pink slowly and carefully emptied the salt from her hand into the water and then upended the shaker. She stirred the water with a branch someone snatched from a bush. After the salt was dissolved, all the Linjeni around them lined up with cupped hands. Each received—as though it were a sacrament—a handful of salt water. And they all, quickly, not to lose a drop, lifted the handful of water to their faces and inhaled, breathing deeply, deeply of the salty solution.

Mrs. Pink was last, and, as she raised her wet face from her cupped hands, the gratitude in her eyes almost made Serena cry. And the dozens of Linjeni crowded around, each eager to press a soft forefinger to Serena's cheek, a thank-you gesture Splinter was picking up already.

When the crowd melted into the shadows again, Mrs. Pink sat down, fondling the salt shaker.

"Salt," said Serena, indicating the shaker.

"*Shreeprill*," said Mrs. Pink.

"*Shreeprill?*" said Serena, her stumbling tongue robbing the word of its liquidness. Mrs. Pink nodded.

"*Shreeprill* good?" asked Serena, groping for an explanation for the just finished scene.

"*Shreeprill* good," said Mrs. Pink. "No *shreeprill*, no Linjeni baby. Doovie—Doovie—" She hesitated, groping. "One Doovie—no baby." She shook her head, unable to bridge the gap.

164

Serena groped after an idea she had almost caught from Mrs. Pink. She pulled up a handful of grass. "Grass," she said. She pulled another handful. "More grass. More. More." She added to the pile.

Mrs. Pink looked from the grass to Serena.

"No *more* Linjeni baby. Doovie—" She separated the grass into piles. "Baby, baby, baby—" She counted down to the last one, lingering tenderly over it. "Doovie."

"Oh," said Serena, "Doovie is the last Linjeni baby? No more?"

Mrs. Pink studied the words and then she nodded. "Yes, yes! No more. No *shreeprill*, no baby."

Serena felt a flutter of wonder. Maybe—maybe this is what the war is over. Maybe they just wanted salt. A world to them. Maybe—

"Salt, *shreeprill*," she said. "More, more more *shreeprill*, Linjeni go home?"

"More more more *shreeprill*, yes," said Mrs. Pink. "Go home, no. No home. Home no good. No water, no *shreeprill*."

"Oh," said Serena. Then thoughtfully, "More Linjeni? More, more, more?"

Mrs. Pink looked at Serena and in the sudden silence the realization that they were, after all, members of enemy camps flared between them. Serena tried to smile. Mrs. Pink looked over at Splinter and Doovie, who were happily sampling everything in the picnic basket. Mrs. Pink relaxed, and then she said, "No more Linjeni." She gestured toward the crowded landing field. "Linjeni." She pressed her hands, palm to palm, her shoulders sagging. "No more Linjeni."

Serena sat dazed, thinking what this would mean to Earth's

High Command. No more Linjeni of the terrible, devastating weapons. No more than those that had landed—no waiting alien world ready to send reinforcements when these ships were gone. When these were gone—no more Linjeni. All that Earth had to do now was wipe out these ships, taking the heavy losses that would be inevitable, and they would win the war—and wipe out a race.

The Linjeni must have come seeking asylum—or demanding it. Neighbors who were afraid to ask—or hadn't been given time to ask. How had the war started? Who fired upon whom? Did anyone know?

Serena took uncertainty home with her, along with the empty picnic basket. *Tell, tell, tell*, whispered her feet through the grass up the hill. *Tell and the war will end*. But how? she cried out to herself. By wiping them out or giving them a home? Which? Which?

Kill, kill, kill grated her feet across the graveled patio edge. *Kill the aliens—no common ground—not human—all our hallowed dead*.

But what about *their* hallowed dead? All falling, the flaming ships—the homeseekers—the dispossessed—the childless?

Serena settled Splinter with a new puzzle and a picture book and went into the bedroom. She sat on the bed and stared at herself in the mirror.

But give them salt water and they'll increase—all our oceans, even if they said they didn't want them. Increase and increase and take the world—push us out—trespass—oppress—

But their men—our men. They've been meeting for over

166

a week and can't agree. Of course they can't! They're afraid of betraying themselves to each other. Neither knows anything about the other, really. They aren't trying to find out anything really important. I'll bet not one of our men know the Linjeni can close their noses and fold their ears. And not one of the Linjeni knows we sprinkle their life on our food.

Serena had no idea how long she sat there, but Splinter finally found her and insisted on supper and then Serena insisted on bed for him.

She was nearly mad with indecision when Thorn finally got home.

"Well," he said, dropping wearily into his chair. "It's almost over."

"Over!" cried Serena, hope flaring. "Then you've reached—"

"Stalemate, impasse," said Thorn heavily. "Our meeting tomorrow is the last. One final 'no' from each side and it's over. Back to bloodletting."

"Oh, Thorn, no!" Serena pressed her clenched fist to her mouth. "We can't kill any more of them! It's inhuman—it's—"

"It's self-defense." Thorn's voice was sharp with exasperated displeasure. "Please, not tonight, Rena. Spare me your idealistic ideas. Heaven knows we're inexperienced enough in warlike negotiations without having to cope with suggestions that we make cute pets out of our enemies. We're in a war and we've got it to win. Let the Linjeni get a wedge in and they'll swarm the Earth like flies!"

"No, no!" whispered Serena, her own secret fears sending

the tears flooding down her face. "They wouldn't! They wouldn't! Would they?"

Long after Thorn's sleeping breath whispered in the darkness beside her, she lay awake, staring at the invisible ceiling. Carefully she put the words up before her on the slate of the darkness.

Tell—the war will end.
Either we will help the Linjeni—or wipe them out.
Don't tell. The conference will break up. The war will go on.
We will have heavy losses—and wipe the Linjeni out.
Mrs. Pink trusted me.
Splinter loves Doovie. Doovie loves him.

Then the little candle flame of prayer that had so nearly burned out in her torment flared brightly again and she slept.

Next morning she sent Splinter to play with Doovie. "Play by the goldfish pond," she said. "I'll be along soon."

"Okay, Mommie," said Splinter. "Will you bring some cake?" Slyly, "Doovie isn't a-miliar with cake."

Serena laughed. "A certain little Splinter is a-miliar with cake, though! You run along, greedy!" And she boosted him out of the door with a slap on the rear.

" 'By, Mommie," he called back.

" 'By, dear. Be good."

"I will."

Serena watched until he disappeared down the slope of the

hill, then she smoothed her hair and ran her tongue over her lips. She started for the bedroom, but turned suddenly and went to the front door. If she had to face even her own eyes, her resolution would waver and dissolve. She stood, hand on knob, watching the clock inch around until an interminable fifteen minutes had passed—Splinter safely gone—then she snatched the door open and left.

Her smile took her out of the Quarters Area to the Administration Building. Her brisk assumption of authority and destination took her to the conference wing and there her courage failed her. She lurked out of sight of the guards, almost wringing her hands in indecision. Then she straightened the set of her skirt, smoothed her hair, dredged a smile up from some hidden source of strength, and tiptoed out into the hall.

She felt like a butterfly pinned to the wall by the instant unwinking attention of the guards. She gestured silence with a finger to her lips and tiptoed up to them.

"Hello, Turner. Hi, Franiveri," she whispered.

The two exchanged looks and Turner said hoarsely, "You aren't supposed to be here, ma'am. Better go."

"I know I'm not," she said, looking guilty—with no effort at all. "But Turner, I—I just want to see a Linjeni." She hurried on before Turner's open mouth could form a word. "Oh, I've seen pictures of them, but I'd like awfully to see a real one. Can't I have even one little peek?" She slipped closer to the door. "Look!" she cried softly. "It's even ajar a little already!"

"Supposed to be," rasped Turner. "Orders. But ma'am, we can't—"

169

"Just one peek?" she pleaded, putting her thumb in the crack of the door. "I won't make a sound."

She coaxed the door open a little farther, her hand creeping inside, fumbling for the knob, the little button.

"But ma'am, you couldn't see 'em from here anyway."

Quicker than thought, Serena jerked the door open and darted in, pushing the little button and slamming the door to with what seemed to her a thunder that vibrated through the whole building. Breathlessly, afraid to think, she sped through the anteroom and into the conference room. She came to a scared skidding stop, her hands tight on the back of a chair, every eye in the room on her. Thorn, almost unrecognizable in his armor of authority and severity, stood up abruptly.

"Serena!" he said, his voice cracking with incredulity. Then he sat down again, hastily.

Serena circled the table, refusing to meet the eyes that bored into her—blue eyes, brown eyes, black eyes, yellow eyes, green eyes, lavender eyes. She turned at the foot of the table and looked fearfully up the shining expanse.

"Gentlemen." Her voice was almost inaudible. She cleared her throat. "Gentlemen." She saw General Worsham getting ready to speak—his face harshly unfamiliar with the weight of his position. She pressed her hands to the polished table and leaned forward hastily.

"You're going to quit, aren't you? You're giving up!" The translators bent to their mikes and their lips moved to hers. "What have you been talking about all this time? Guns? Battles? Casualty lists? We'll-do-this-to-you-if-you-do-that-to-us? I don't know! . . ." she cried, shaking her head tightly, almost

shuddering. "I don't know what goes on at high level conference tables. All I know is that I've been teaching Mrs. Pink
to knit, and how to cut a lemon pie . . ." She could see the
bewildered interpreters thumbing their manuals. ". . . and already I know why they're here and what they want!" Pursing
her lips, she half whistled, half trilled in her halting Linjeni,
"Doovie baby. No more Linjeni babies!"

One of the Linjeni started at Doovie's name and stood up
slowly, his lavender bulk towering over the table. Serena saw
the interpreters thumbing frantically again. She knew they
were looking for a translation of the Linjeni "baby." Babies
had no place in a military conference.

The Linjeni spoke slowly, but Serena shook her head. "I
don't know enough Linjeni."

There was a whisper at her shoulder. "What do you know
of Doovie?" And a pair of earphones was pushed into her
hands. She adjusted them with trembling fingers. Why were
they letting her talk? Why was General Worsham sitting there
letting her break into the conference like this?

"I know Doovie," she said breathlessly. "I know Doovie's
mother, too. Doovie plays with Splinter, my son—my little
son." She twisted her fingers, dropping her head at the murmur
that arose around the table. The Linjeni spoke again and the
metallic murmur of the earphones gave her the translation.
"What is the color of Doovie's mother?"

"Pink," said Serena.

Again the scurry for a word—pink—pink. Finally Serena
turned up the hem of her skirt and displayed the hem of her
slip—rose pink. The Linjeni sat down again, nodding.

171

"Serena." General Worsham spoke as quietly as though it were just another lounging evening on the patio. "What do you want?"

Serena's eyes wavered and then her chin lifted.

"Thorn said today would be the last day. That it was to be 'no' on both sides. That we and the Linjeni have no common meeting ground, no basis for agreement on anything."

"And you think we have?" General Worsham's voice cut gently through the stir at the naked statement of thoughts and attitudes so carefully concealed.

"I know we do. Our alikenesses outweigh our differences so far that it's just foolish to sit here all this time, shaking our differences at each other and not finding out a thing about our likenesses. We are fundamentally the same—the same—" She faltered. "Under God we are all the same." And she knew with certainty that the translators wouldn't find God's name in their books. "I think we ought to let them eat our salt and bread and make them welcome!" She half smiled and said, "The word for salt is *shreeprill*."

There was a smothered rush of whistling from the Linjeni, and the lavender Linjeni half rose from his chair but subsided.

General Worsham glanced at the Linjeni speculatively and pursed his lips. "But there are ramifications—" he began.

"Ramifications!" spat Serena. "There are no ramifications that can't resolve themselves if two peoples really know each other!"

She glanced around the table, noting with sharp relief that Thorn's face had softened.

"Come with me!" she urged. "Come and see Doovie and

172

Splinter together—Linjeni young and ours, who haven't learned suspicion and fear and hate and prejudice yet. Declare a—a—recess or a truce or whatever is necessary and come with me. After you see the children and see Mrs. Pink knitting and we talk this matter over like members of a family—well, if you still think you have to fight after that, then—" She spread her hands.

Her knees shook so as they started downhill that Thorn had to help her walk.

"Oh, Thorn," she whispered, almost sobbing. "I didn't think they would. I thought they'd shoot me or lock me up or—"

"We don't want war. I told you that," he murmured. "We're ready to grab at straws, even in the guise of snippy females who barge in on solemn councils and display their slips!" Then his lips tightened. "How long has this been going on?"

"For Splinter, a couple of weeks. For me, a little more than a week."

"Why didn't you tell me?"

"I tried—twice. You wouldn't listen. I was too scared to insist. Besides, you know what your reaction would have been."

Thorn had no words until they neared the foot of the hill; then he said, "How come you know so much? What makes you think you can solve—"

Serena choked back a hysterical laugh. "I took eggs to a picnic!"

And then they were standing, looking down at the hole under the fence.

"Splinter found the way," Serena defended. "I made it bigger, but you'll have to get down—flat."

She dropped to the sand and wiggled under. She crouched on the other side, her knees against her chest, her clasped hands pressed against her mouth, and waited. There was a long minute of silence and then a creak and a grunt and Serena bit her lips as General Worsham inched under the fence, flat on the sand, catching and jerking free halfway through. But her amusement changed to admiration as she realized that even covered with dust, scrambling awkwardly to his feet and beating his rumpled clothing, he possessed dignity and strength that made her deeply thankful that he was the voice of Earth in this time of crisis.

One by one the others crawled under, the Linjeni sandwiched between the other men and Thorn bringing up the rear. Motioning silence, she led them to the thicket of bushes that screened one side of the goldfish pond.

Doovie and Splinter were leaning over the edge of the pond.

"There it is!" cried Splinter, leaning perilously and pointing. "Way down there on the bottom and it's my best marble. Would your Mommie care if you got it for me?"

Doovie peered down. "Marble go in water."

"That's what I said," cried Splinter impatiently. "And you can shut your nose . . ." He put his finger to the black, glistening button. ". . . and fold your ears." He flicked them with his forefinger and watched them fold. "Gee!" he said admiringly. "I wish I could do that."

"Doovie go in water?" asked Doovie.

"Yes," nodded Splinter. "It's my good taw, and you won't even have to put on swimming trunks—you got fur."

174

Doovie shucked out of his brief clothing and slid down into the pond. He bobbed back up, his hand clenched.

"Gee, thanks." Splinter held out his hand and Doovie carefully turned his hand over and Splinter closed his. Then he shrieked and flung his hand out. "You mean old thing!" yelled Splinter. "Give me my marble! That was a slippy old fish!" He leaned over, scuffling, trying to reach Doovie's other hand. There was a slither and a splash and Splinter and Doovie disappeared under the water.

Serena caught her breath and had started forward when Doovie's anxious face bobbed to the surface again. He yanked and tugged at the sputtering, coughing Splinter and tumbled him out onto the grass. Doovie squatted by Splinter, patting his back and alternately whistling dolefully through his nose and talking apologetic-sounding Linjeni.

Splinter coughed and dug his fists into his eyes.

"Golly, golly!" he said, spatting his hands against his wet jersey. "Mommie'll sure be mad. My clean clothes all wet. Where's my marble, Doovie?"

Doovie scrambled to his feet and went back to the pond. Splinter started to follow, then he cried, "Oh, Doovie, where did that poor little fish go? It'll die if it's out of the water. My guppy did."

"Fish?" asked Doovie.

"Yes," said Splinter, holding out his hand as he searched the grass with intent eyes. "The slippy little fish that wasn't my marble."

The two youngsters scrambled around in the grass until Doovie whistled and cried out triumphantly, "Fish!" and scooped it up in his hands and rushed it back to the pond.

"There," said Splinter. "Now it won't die. Looky, it's swimming away!"

Doovie slid into the pond again and retrieved the lost marble.

"Now," said Splinter. "Watch me and I'll show you how to shoot."

The bushes beyond the two absorbed boys parted and Mrs. Pink stepped out. She smiled at the children and then she saw the silent group on the other side of the clearing. Her eyes widened and she gave an astonished whistle. The two boys looked up and followed the direction of her eyes.

"Daddy!" yelled Splinter. "Did you come to play?" And he sped, arms outstretched, to Thorn, arriving only a couple of steps ahead of Doovie, who was whistling excitedly and rushing to greet the tall lavender Linjeni.

Serena felt a sudden choke of laughter at how alike Thorn and the Linjeni looked, trying to greet their offspring adequately and still retain their dignity.

Mrs. Pink came hesitantly to the group to stand in the circle of Serena's arm. Splinter had swarmed up Thorn, hugged him with thoroughness, and slid down again. "Hi, General Worsham!" he said, extending a muddy hand in a belated remembrance of his manners. "Hey, Daddy, I'm showing Doovie how to play marbles, but you can shoot better'n I can. You come show him how."

"Well—" said Thorn, glancing uncomfortably at General Worsham.

General Worsham was watching the Linjeni as Doovie whistled and fluted over a handful of bright-colored glassies. He quirked an eyebrow at Thorn and then at the rest of the group.

"I suggest a recess," he said. "In order that we may examine new matters that have been brought to our attention."

Serena felt herself getting all hollow inside, and she turned her face away so Mrs. Pink wouldn't see her cry. But Mrs. Pink was too interested in the colorful marbles to see Serena's gathering, hopeful tears.

Murray Leinster

Keyhole

There are often two ways to look at things. Sometimes
both approaches are worthwhile.

When they brought Butch into the station in Tycho Crater
he seemed to shrivel as the gravity coils in the air lock went
on. He was impossible to begin with. He was all big eyes and
skinny arms and legs, and he was very young and he didn't
need air to breathe. Worden saw him as a limp bundle of
bristly fur and terrified eyes as his captors handed him over.

"Are you crazy?" demanded Worden angrily. "Bringing him
in like this? Would you take a human baby into eight gravities?
Get out of the way!"

He rushed for the nursery that had been made ready for
somebody like Butch. There was a rebuilt dwelling-cave on
one side. The other side was a human schoolroom. And under
the nursery the gravity coils had been turned off so that in that
room things had only the weight that was proper to them on
the Moon.

The rest of the station had coils to bring everything up to

normal weight for Earth. Otherwise the staff of the station would be seasick most of the time. Butch was in the Earth-gravity part of the station when he was delivered, and he couldn't lift a furry spindly paw.

In the nursery, though, it was different. Worden put him on the floor. Worden was the uncomfortable one there—his weight only twenty pounds instead of a normal hundred and sixty. He swayed and reeled as a man does on the Moon without gravity coils to steady him.

But that was the normal thing to Butch. He uncurled himself and suddenly flashed across the nursery to the reconstructed dwelling-cave. It was a pretty good job, that cave. There were the five-foot chipped rocks shaped like dunce caps, found in all residences of Butch's race. There was the rocking stone on its base of other flattened rocks. But the spear stones were fastened down with wire in case Butch got ideas.

Butch streaked in to these familiar objects. He swarmed up one of the dunce-cap stones and locked his arms and legs about its top, clinging close. Then he was still. Worden regarded him. Butch was motionless for minutes, seeming to take in as much as possible of his surroundings without moving even his eyes.

Suddenly his head moved. He took in more of his environment. Then he stirred a third time and seemed to look at Worden with an extraordinary intensity—whether of fear or pleading Worden could not tell.

"Hmm," said Worden, "so that's what those stones are for! Perches or beds or roosts, eh? I'm your nurse, fella. We're playing a dirty trick on you but we can't help it."

He knew Butch couldn't understand, but he talked to him

179

as a man does talk to a dog or a baby. It isn't sensible, but it's necessary.

"We're going to raise you up to be a traitor to your kinfolk," he said with some grimness. "I don't like it, but it has to be done. So I'm going to be very kind to you as part of the conspiracy. Real kindness would suggest that I kill you instead—but I can't do that."

Butch stared at him, unblinking and motionless. He looked something like an Earth monkey but not too much so. He was completely impossible but he looked pathetic.

Worden said bitterly, "You're in your nursery, Butch. Make yourself at home!"

He went out and closed the door behind him. Outside he glanced at the video screens that showed the interior of the nursery from four different angles. Butch remained still for a long time. Then he slipped down to the floor. This time he ignored the dwelling-cave of the nursery.

He went interestedly to the human-culture part. He examined everything there with his oversized soft eyes. He touched everything with his incredibly handlike tiny paws. But his touches were tentative. Nothing was actually disturbed when he finished his examination.

He went swiftly back to the dunce-cap rock, swarmed up it, locked his arms and legs about it again, blinked rapidly, and seemed to go to sleep. He remained motionless with closed eyes until Worden grew tired of watching him and moved away.

The whole affair was preposterous and infuriating. The first men to land on the Moon knew that it was a dead world. The astronomers had been saying so for a hundred years, and the first and second expeditions to reach Luna from Earth found nothing to contradict the theory.

But a man from the third expedition saw something moving among the upflung rocks of the Moon's landscape and he shot it and the existence of Butch's kind was discovered. It was inconceivable, of course, that there should be living creatures where there was neither air nor water. But Butch's folk did live under exactly those conditions.

The dead body of the first living creature killed on the Moon was carried back to Earth and biologists grew indignant. Even with a specimen to dissect and study they were inclined to insist that there simply wasn't any such creature. So the fourth and fifth and sixth lunar expeditions hunted Butch's relatives very earnestly for further specimens for the advancement of science.

The sixth expedition lost two men whose spacesuits were punctured by what seemed to be weapons while they were hunting. The seventh expedition was wiped out to the last man. Butch's relatives evidently didn't like being shot as biological specimens.

It wasn't until the tenth expedition of four ships established a base in Tycho Crater that men had any assurance of being able to land on the Moon and get away again. Even then the staff of the station felt as if it were under permanent siege.

Worden made his report to Earth. A baby lunar creature had been captured by a tractor party and brought into Tycho Station. A nursery was ready and the infant was there now, alive. He seemed to be uninjured. He seemed not to mind an

181

environment of breathable air for which he had no use. He was active and apparently curious and his intelligence was marked.

There was so far no clue to what he ate—if he ate at all—though he had a mouth like the other collected specimens and the toothlike concretions which might serve as teeth. Worden would, of course, continue to report in detail. At the moment he was allowing Butch to accustom himself to his new surroundings.

He settled down in the recreation room to scowl at his companion scientists and try to think, despite the program beamed on radar frequency from Earth. He definitely didn't like his job, but he knew that it had to be done. Butch had to be domesticated. He had to be persuaded that he was a human being, so human beings could find out how to exterminate his kind.

It had been observed before, on Earth, that a kitten raised with a litter of puppies came to consider itself a dog and that even pet ducks came to prefer human society to that of their own species. Some talking birds of high intelligence appeared to be convinced that they were people and acted that way. If Butch reacted similarly he would become a traitor to his kind for the benefit of man. And it was necessary!

Men had to have the Moon, and that was all there was to it. Gravity on the Moon was one eighth that of gravity on Earth. A rocket ship could make the Moon voyage and carry a cargo, but no ship yet built could carry fuel for a trip to Mars or Venus if it started out from Earth.

With a fueling stop on the Moon, though, the matter was

simple. Eight drums of rocket fuel on the Moon weighed no more than one on Earth. A ship itself weighed only one eighth as much on Luna. So a rocket that took off from Earth with ten drums of fuel could stop at a fuel base on the Moon and soar away again with two hundred, and sometimes more.

With the Moon as a fueling base men could conquer the solar system. Without the Moon, mankind was earthbound. Men had to have the Moon!

But Butch's relatives prevented it. By normal experience there could not be life on an airless desert with such monstrous extremes of heat and cold as the Moon's surface experienced. But there was life there. Butch's kinfolk did not breathe oxygen. Apparently they ate it in some mineral combination and it interacted with other minerals in their bodies to yield heat and energy.

Men thought squids peculiar because their bloodstream used copper in place of iron, but Butch and his kindred seemed to have complex carbon compounds in place of both. They were intelligent in some fashion, it was clear. They used tools, they chipped stone, and they had long, needlelike stone crystals which they threw as weapons.

No metals, of course, for lack of fire to smelt them. There couldn't be fire without air. But Worden reflected that in ancient days some experimenters had melted metals and set wood ablaze with mirrors concentrating the heat of the sun. With the naked sunlight of the Moon's surface, not tempered by air and clouds, Butch's folk could have metals if they only contrived mirrors and curved them properly like the mirrors of telescopes on Earth.

Worden had an odd sensation just then. He looked around sharply as if somebody had made a sudden movement. But the video screen merely displayed a comedian back on Earth, wearing a funny hat. Everybody looked at the screen.

As Worden watched, the comedian was smothered in a mass of soapsuds and the studio audience two hundred and thirty thousand miles away squealed and applauded the exquisite humor of the scene. In the Moon station in Tycho Crater somehow it was less than comical.

Worden got up and shook himself. He went to look again at the screens that showed the interior of the nursery. Butch was motionless on the absurd cone-shaped stone. His eyes were closed. He was simply a furry, pathetic little bundle, stolen from the airless wastes outside to be bred into a traitor to his race.

Worden went to his cabin and turned in. Before he slept, though, he reflected that there was still some hope for Butch. Nobody understood his metabolism. Nobody could guess at what he ate. Butch might starve to death. If he did, he would be lucky. But it was Worden's job to prevent it.

Butch's relatives were at war with men. The tractors that crawled away from the station—they went amazingly fast on the Moon—were watched by big-eyed furry creatures from rock crevices and from behind the boulders that dotted the lunar landscape.

Needle-sharp throwing stones flicked through emptiness. They splintered on the tractor bodies and on the tractor ports, but sometimes they jammed or broke a tread and then the tractor had to stop. Somebody had to go out and clear things or make repairs. And then a storm of throwing stones poured upon him.

A needle-pointed stone, traveling a hundred feet a second, hit just as hard on Luna as it did on Earth—and it traveled farther. Spacesuits were punctured. Men died. Now tractor treads were being armored and special repair-suits were under construction, made of hardened steel plates.

Men who reached the Moon in rocket ships were having to wear armor like medieval knights and men-at-arms! There was a war on. A traitor was needed. And Butch was elected to be that traitor.

When Worden went into the nursery again—the days and nights on the Moon are two weeks long apiece, so men ignored such matters inside the station—Butch leaped for the dunce-cap stone and clung to its top. He had been fumbling around the rocking stone. It still swayed back and forth on its plate. Now he seemed to try to squeeze himself to unity with the stone spire, his eyes staring enigmatically at Worden.

"I don't know whether we'll get anywhere or not," said Worden conversationally. "Maybe you'll put up a fight if I touch you. But we'll see."

He reached out his hand. The small furry body—neither hot nor cold but the temperature of the air in the station—resisted desperately. But Butch was very young. Worden peeled him loose and carried him across the room to the human schoolroom equipment. Butch curled up, staring fearfully.

"I'm playing dirty," said Worden, "by being nice to you, Butch. Here's a toy."

Butch stirred in his grasp. His eyes blinked rapidly. Worden put him down and wound up a tiny mechanical toy. It moved. Butch watched intently. When it stopped he looked back at Worden. Worden wound it up again. Again Butch watched. When it ran down a second time the tiny handlike paw reached out.

With an odd tentativeness, Butch tried to turn the winding key. He was not strong enough. After an instant he went loping across to the dwelling-cave. The winding key was a metal ring. Butch fitted that over a throw-stone point, and twisted the toy about. He wound it up. He put the toy on the floor and watched it work. Worden's jaw dropped.

"Brains!" he said wryly. "Too bad, Butch! You know the principle of the lever. At a guess you've an eight-year-old human brain! I'm sorry for you, fella!"

At the regular communication hour he made his report to Earth. Butch was teachable. He only had to see a thing done once—or at most twice—to be able to repeat the motions involved.

"And," said Worden, carefully detached, "he isn't afraid of me now. He understands that I intend to be friendly. While I was carrying him I talked to him. He felt the vibration of my chest from my voice.

"Just before I left him I picked him up and talked to him again. He looked at my mouth as it moved and put his paw on my chest to feel the vibrations. I put his paw at my throat. The vibrations are clearer there. He seemed fascinated. I don't know how you'd rate his intelligence but it's above that of a human baby."

Then he said with even greater detachment, "I am disturbed.

186

If you must know, I don't like the idea of exterminating his kind. They have tools, they have intelligence. I think we should try to communicate with them in some way—try to make friends—stop killing them for dissection."

The communicator was silent for the second and a half it took his voice to travel to Earth and the second and a half it took to come back. Then the recording clerk's voice said briskly, "Very good, Mr. Worden! Your voice was very clear!"

Worden shrugged his shoulders. The lunar station in Tycho was a highly official enterprise. The staff on the Moon had to be competent—and besides, political appointees did not want to risk their precious lives—but the Earth end of the business of the Space Exploration Bureau was run by the sort of people who do get on official payrolls. Worden felt sorry for Butch—and for Butch's relatives.

In a later lesson session Worden took an empty coffee tin into the nursery. He showed Butch that its bottom vibrated when he spoke into it, just as his throat did. Butch experimented busily. He discovered for himself that it had to be pointed at Worden to catch the vibrations.

Worden was unhappy. He would have preferred Butch to be a little less rational. But for the next lesson he presented Butch with a really thin metal diaphragm stretched across a hoop. Butch caught the idea at once.

When Worden made his next report to Earth he felt angry.

"Butch has no experience of sound as we have, of course," he said curtly. "There's no air on the Moon. But sound travels through rocks. He's sensitive to vibrations in solid objects just as a deaf person can feel the vibrations of a dance floor if the music is loud enough.

"Maybe Butch's kind has a language or a code of sounds sent through the rock underfoot. They do communicate somehow! And if they've brains and a means of communication they aren't animals and shouldn't be exterminated for our convenience!"

He stopped. The chief biologist of the Space Exploration Bureau was at the other end of the communication beam then. After the necessary pause for distance his voice came blandly.

"Splendid, Worden! Splendid reasoning! But we have to take the longer view. Exploration of Mars and Venus is a very popular idea with the public. If we are to have funds—and the appropriations come up for a vote shortly—we have to make progress toward the nearer planets. The public demands it. Unless we can begin work on a refueling base on the Moon, public interest will cease!"

Worden said urgently, "Suppose I send some pictures of Butch? He's very human, sir! He's extraordinarily appealing! He has personality! A reel or two of Butch at his lessons ought to be popular!"

Again that irritating wait while his voice traveled a quarter-million miles at the speed of light and the wait for the reply.

"The—ah—lunar creatures, Worden," said the chief biologist regretfully, "have killed a number of men who have been publicized as martyrs to science. We cannot give favorable publicity to creatures that have killed men!" Then he added blandly, "But you are progressing splendidly, Worden— *splendidly*! Carry on!"

His image faded from the video screen. Worden said naughty words as he turned away. He'd come to like Butch. Butch trusted him. Butch now slid down from that crazy perch of his and came rushing to his arms every time he entered the nursery.

Butch was ridiculously small—no more than eighteen inches high. He was preposterously light and fragile in his nursery, where only Moon gravity was obtained. And Butch was such an earnest little creature, so soberly absorbed in everything that Worden showed him!

He was still fascinated by the phenomena of sound. Humming or singing—even Worden's humming and singing—entranced him. When Worden's lips moved now Butch struck an attitude and held up the hoop diaphragm with a tiny finger pressed to it to catch the vibrations Worden's voice made.

Now, too, when he grasped an idea Worden tried to convey, he tended to swagger. He became more human in his actions with every session of human contact. Once, indeed, Worden looked at the video screens which spied on Butch and saw him—all alone—solemnly going through every gesture and every movement Worden had made. He was pretending to give a lesson to an imaginary still-tinier companion. He was pretending to be Worden, apparently for his own satisfaction!

Worden felt a lump in his throat. He was enormously fond of the little mite. It was painful that he had just left Butch to help in the construction of a vibrator-microphone device which would transfer his voice to rock vibrations and simultaneously pick up any other vibrations that might be made in return.

If the members of Butch's race did communicate by tapping

on rocks, or the like, men could eavesdrop on them—could locate them, could detect ambushes in preparation, and apply mankind's deadly military countermeasures.

Worden hoped the gadget wouldn't work. But it did. When he put it on the floor of the nursery and spoke into the microphone, Butch did feel the vibrations underfoot. He recognized their identity with the vibrations he'd learned to detect in air.

He made a skipping, exultant hop and jump. It was plainly the uttermost expression of satisfaction. And then his tiny foot pattered and scratched furiously on the floor. It made a peculiar scratchy tapping noise which the microphone picked up. Butch watched Worden's face, making the sounds which were like highly elaborated footfalls.

"No dice, Butch," said Worden unhappily. "I can't understand it. But it looks as if you've started your treason already. This'll help wipe out some of your folks."

He reported it reluctantly to the head of the station. Microphones were immediately set into the rocky crater floor outside the station and others were made ready for exploring parties to use for the detection of Moon creatures near them. Oddly enough, the microphones by the station yielded results right away.

It was near sunset. Butch had been captured near the middle of the three-hundred-and-thirty-four-hour lunar day. In all the hours between—a week by Earth time—he had had no nourishment of any sort. Worden had conscientiously offered him every edible and inedible substance in the station. Then at least one sample of every mineral in the station collection.

Butch regarded them all with interest but without appetite. Worden—liking Butch—expected him to die of starvation and thought it a good idea. Better then encompassing the death of all his race, anyhow. And it did seem to him that Butch was beginning to show a certain sluggishness, a certain lack of bounce and energy. He thought it was weakness from hunger.

Sunset progressed. Yard by yard, fathom by fathom, half mile by half mile, the shadows of the miles-high western walls of Tycho crept across the crater floor. There came a time when only the central hump had sunlight. Then the shadow began to creep up the eastern walls. Presently the last thin jagged line of light would vanish and the colossal cup of the crater would be filled to overflowing with the night.

Worden watched the incandescent sunlight growing even narrower on the cliffs. He would see no other sunlight for two weeks' Earth time. Then abruptly an alarm bell rang. It clanged stridently, furiously. Doors hissed shut, dividing the station into airtight sections.

Loudspeakers snapped, *"Noises in the rock outside! Sounds like Moon creatures talking nearby! They may plan an attack! Everbody into spacesuits and get guns ready!"*

At just that instant the last thin sliver of sunshine disappeared. Worden thought instantly of Butch. There was no spacesuit to fit him. Then he grimaced a little. Butch didn't need a spacesuit.

Worden got into the clumsy outfit. The lights dimmed. The harsh airless space outside the station was suddenly bathed in light. The multimillion-lumen beam, made to guide rocket ships to a landing even at night, was turned on to expose any creatures with designs on its owners. It was startling to see how

191

little space was really lighted by the beam and how much of stark blackness spread on beyond.

The loudspeaker snapped again, *"Two Moon creatures! Running away! They're zigzagging! Anybody who wants to take a shot—"* The voice paused. It didn't matter. Nobody is a crack shot in a spacesuit. *"They left something behind!"* said the voice in the loudspeaker. It was sharp and uneasy.

"I'll take a look at that," said Worden. His own voice startled him but he was depressed. "I've got a hunch what it is."

Minutes later he went out through the air lock. He moved lightly despite the cumbrous suit he wore. There were two other staff members with him. All three were armed and the searchlight beam stabbed here and there erratically to expose any relative of Butch who might try to approach them in the darkness.

With the light at his back Worden could see that trillions of stars looked down upon Luna. The zenith was filled with infinitesimal specks of light of every conceivable color. The familiar constellations burned ten times as brightly as on Earth. And Earth itself hung nearly overhead. It was three-quarters full—a monstrous bluish giant in the sky, four times the Moon's diameter, its ice caps and continents mistily to be seen.

Worden went forebodingly to the object left behind by Butch's kin. He wasn't much surprised when he saw what it was. It was a rocking stone on its plate with a fine impalpable dust on the plate, as if something had been crushed under the egg-shaped upper stone acting as a mill.

Worden said sourly into his helmet microphone, "It's a present for Butch. His kinfolk know he was captured alive.

They suspect he's hungry. They've left some grub for him of the kind he wants or needs most."

That was plainly what it was. It did not make Worden feel proud. A baby—Butch—had been kidnaped by the enemies of its race. That baby was a prisoner and its captors would have nothing with which to feed it. So someone, greatly daring— Worden wondered somberly if it was Butch's father and mother— had risked their lives to leave food for him with a rocking stone to tag it for recognition as food.

"It's a dirty shame," said Worden bitterly. "All right! Let's carry it back. Careful not to spill the powdered stuff!"

His lack of pride was emphasized when Butch fell upon the unidentified powder with marked enthusiasm. Tiny pinch by tiny pinch Butch consumed it with an air of vast satisfaction. Worden felt ashamed.

"You're getting treated pretty rough, Butch," said Worden. "What I've already learned from you will cost a good many hundred of your folks' lives. And they're taking chances to feed you! I'm making you a traitor and myself a scoundrel."

Butch thoughtfully held up the hoop diaphragm to catch the voice vibrations in the air. He was small and furry and absorbed. He decided that he could pick up sounds better from the rock underfoot. He pressed the communicator microphone on Worden. He waited.

"No!" said Worden roughly. "Your people are too human. Don't let me find out any more, Butch. Be smart and play dumb!"

But Butch didn't. It wasn't very long before Worden was

teaching him to read. Oddly, though, the rock microphones that had given the alarm at the station didn't help the tractor parties at all. Butch's kinfolk seemed to vanish from the neighborhood of the station altogether. Of course if that kept up, the construction of a fuel base could be begun and the actual extermination of the species carried out later. But the reports on Butch were suggesting other possibilities.

"If your folks stay vanished," Worden told Butch, "it'll be all right for a while—and only for a while. I'm being urged to try to get you used to Earth gravity. If I succeed, they'll want you on Earth in a zoo. And if that works—why, they'll be sending other expeditions to get more of your kinfolk to put in other zoos."

Butch watched Worden, motionless.

"And also"—Worden's tone was very grim—"there's some miniature mining machinery coming up by the next rocket. I'm supposed to see if you can learn to run it."

Butch made scratching sounds on the floor. It was unintelligible of course, but it was an expression of interest at least. Butch seemed to enjoy the vibrations of Worden's voice, just as a dog likes to have his master talk to him. Worden grunted.

"We humans class you as an animal, Butch. We tell ourselves that all the animal world should be subject to us. Animals should work for us. If you act too smart we'll hunt down all your relatives and set them to work digging minerals for us. You'll be with them. But I don't want you to work your heart out in a mine, Butch! It's wrong!"

Butch remained quite still. Worden thought sickishly of small furry creatures like Butch driven to labor in airless mines in the Moon's frigid depths. With guards in spacesuits watching lest any try to escape to the freedom they'd known before the coming of men. With guns mounted against revolt. With punishments for rebellion or weariness.

It wouldn't be unprecedented. The Indians in Cuba when the Spanish came . . . Negro slavery in both Americas . . . concentration camps . . .

Butch moved. He put a small furry paw on Worden's knee. Worden scowled at him.

"Bad business," he said harshly. "I'd rather not get fond of you. You're a likable little cuss but your race is doomed. The trouble is that you didn't bother to develop a civilization. And if you had, I suspect we'd have smashed it. We humans aren't what you'd call admirable."

Butch went over to the blackboard. He took a piece of pastel chalk—ordinary chalk was too hard for his Moon-gravity muscles to use—and soberly began to make marks on the slate. The marks formed letters. The letters made words. The words made sense.

YOU, wrote Butch quite incredibly in neat pica lettering, GOOD FRIEND.

He turned his head to stare at Worden. Worden went white. "I haven't taught you those words, Butch!" he said very quietly. "What's up?"

He'd forgotten that his words, to Butch, were merely vibrations in the air or in the floor. He'd forgotten they had no meaning. But Butch seemed to have forgotten it too. He marked soberly:

MY FRIEND GET SPACESUIT. He looked at Worden and marked once more. TAKE ME OUT. I COME BACK WITH YOU.

He looked at Worden with large incongruously soft and

appealing eyes. And Worden's brain seemed to spin inside his skull. After a long time Butch printed again—YES.

Then Worden sat very still indeed. There was only Moon gravity in the nursery and he weighed only one eighth as much as on Earth. But he felt very weak. Then he felt grim.

"Not much else to do, I suppose," he said slowly. "But I'll have to carry you through Earth gravity to the air lock."

He got to his feet. Butch made a little leap up into his arms. He curled up there, staring at Worden's face. Just before Worden stepped through the door Butch reached up a skinny paw and caressed Worden's cheek tentatively.

"Here we go!" said Worden. "The idea was for you to be a traitor. I wonder—"

But with Butch a furry ball, suffering in the multiplied weight Earth gravity imposed upon him, Worden made his way to the air lock. He donned a spacesuit. He went out.

It was near sunrise then. A long time had passed and Earth was now in its last quarter, and the very highest peak of all that made up the crater wall glowed incandescent in the sunshine. But the stars were still quite visible and very bright. Worden walked away from the station, guided by the Earthshine on the ground underfoot.

Three hours later he came back. Butch skipped and hopped beside his spacesuited figure. Behind them came two other figures. They were smaller than Worden but much larger than Butch. They were skinny and furry and they carried a burden. A mile from the station he switched on his suit radio. He called. A startled voice answered in his earphones.

"It's Worden," he said dryly. "I've been out for a walk with

Butch. We visited his family and I've a couple of his cousins with me. They want to pay a visit and present some gifts. Will you let us in without shooting?"

There were exclamations. There was confusion. But Worden went on steadily toward the station while another high peak glowed in sunrise light and a third seemed to burst into incandescence. Dawn was definitely on the way.

The air-lock door opened. The party from the airless Moon went in. When the air lock filled, though, and the gravity coils went on, Butch and his relatives became helpless. They had to be carried to the nursery. There they uncurled themselves and blinked enigmatically at the men who crowded into the room where gravity was normal for the Moon and at the other men who stared in the door.

"I've got a sort of message," said Worden. "Butch and his relatives want to make a deal with us. You'll notice that they've put themselves at our mercy. We can kill all three of them. But they want to make a deal."

The head of the station said uncomfortably, "You've managed two-way communication, Worden?"

"*I* haven't," Worden told him. "*They* have. They've proved to me that they've brains equal to ours. They've been treated as animals and shot as specimens. They've fought back—naturally! But they want to make friends. They say that we can never use the Moon except in spacesuits and in stations like this, and they could never take Earth's gravity. So there's no need for us to be enemies. We can help each other."

The head of the station said dryly, "Plausible enough, but we have to act under orders, Worden. Did you explain that?"

197

"They know," said Worden. "So they've got set to defend themselves if necessary. They've set up smelters to handle metals. They get the heat by sun mirrors, concentrating sunlight. They've even begun to work with gases held in containers. They're not far along with electronics yet, but they've got the theoretic knowledge and they don't need vacuum tubes. They live in a vacuum. They can defend themselves from now on."

The head said mildly, "I've watched Butch, you know, Worden. And you don't look crazy. But if this sort of thing is sprung on the armed forces on Earth there'll be trouble. They've been arguing for armed rocket ships. If your friends start a real war for defense—if they can—maybe rocket warships will be the answer."

Worden nodded.

"Right. But our rockets aren't so good that they can fight this far from a fuel store, and there couldn't be one on the Moon with all of Butch's kinfolk civilized—as they nearly are now and as they certainly will be within the next few weeks. Smart people, these cousins and such of Butch!"

"I'm afraid they'll have to prove it," said the head. "Where'd they get this sudden surge in culture?"

"From us," said Worden. "Smelting from me, I think. Metallurgy and mechanical engineering from the tractor mechanics. Geology—call it lunology here—mostly from you."

"Hows that?" demanded the head.

"Think of something you'd like Butch to do," said Worden grimly, "and then watch him."

The head stared and then looked at Butch. Butch—small

198

and furry and swaggering—stood up and bowed profoundly from the waist. One paw was placed where his heart could be. The other made a grandiose sweeping gesture. He straightened up and strutted, then climbed swiftly into Worden's lap and put a skinny furry arm about his neck.

"That bow," said the head, very pale, "is what I had in mind. You mean—"

"Just so," said Worden. "Butch's ancestors had no air to make noises in for speech. So they developed telepathy. In time, to be sure, they worked out something like music—sounds carried through rock. But like our music it doesn't carry meaning. They communicate directly from mind to mind. Only we can't pick up communications from them and they can from us."

"They read our minds!" said the head. He licked his lips. "And when we first shot them for specimens, they were trying to communicate. Now they fight."

"Naturally," said Worden. "Wouldn't we? They've been picking our brains. They can put up a terrific battle now. They could wipe out this station without trouble. They let us stay so they could learn from us. Now they want to trade."

"We have to report to Earth," said the head slowly, "but—"

"They brought along some samples," said Worden. "They'll swap diamonds, weight for weight, for records. They like our music. They'll trade emeralds for textbooks—they can read now! And they'll set up an atomic pile and swap plutonium for other things they'll think of later. Trading on that basis should be cheaper than a war!"

"Yes," said the head. "It should. That's the sort of argument men will listen to. But how—"

"Butch," said Worden ironically. "Just Butch! We didn't capture him—they planted him on us! He stayed in the station and picked our brains and relayed the stuff to his relatives. We wanted to learn about them, remember? It's like the story of the psychologist . . ."

There's a story about a psychologist who was studying the intelligence of a chimpanzee. He led the chimp into a room full of toys, went out, closed the door and put his eye to the keyhole to see what the chimp was doing. He found himself gazing into a glittering, interested brown eye only inches from his own. The chimp was looking through the keyhole to see what the psychologist was doing.

James E. Gunn

Kindergarten

Is the world messed up? Well, maybe this story tells us why.

First day—

Teacher told my parent that I am the slowest youngster in my class, but today I made a star in the third quadrant of kindergarten.

Teacher was surprised. Teacher tried to hide it and said the solar phoenix reaction is artistic, but is it practical?

I don't care. I think it's pretty.

Second day—

Today I made planets: four big ones, two middle-sized ones, and three little ones. Teacher laughed and said why did I make so many when all but three were too hot or too cold to support life and the big ones were too massive and poisonous for any use at all.

Teacher doesn't understand. There is more to creation than mere usefulness.

The rings around the sixth planet are beautiful.

Third day—

Today I created life. I begin to understand why my people place creation above all else.

I have heard the philosophers discussing the purpose of existence, but I thought it was merely age. Before today, joy was enough: to have fun with the other kids, to speed through endless space, to explode some unstable star into a nova, to flee before the outrage of some adult—this would fill eternity.

Now I know better. Life must have a function.

Teacher was right: only two of the middle-sized planets and one of the little ones were suitable for life. I made life for all three, but only on the third planet from the sun was it really successful.

I have given it only one function: survive!

Fourth day—

The third planet has absorbed all my interest. The soupy seas are churning with life.

Today I introduced a second function: multiply!

The forms developing in the seas are increasingly complex.

The kids are calling me to come and play, but I'm not going.

This is more fun.

Fifth day—

Time after time I stranded sea-creatures on the land and

kept them alive long past the time when they should have died. At last I succeeded. Some of them have adapted.

I was right. The sea is definitely an inhibiting factor.

The success of the land-creatures is pleasing.

Sixth day—

Everything I did before today was nothing. Today I created intelligence.

I added a third function: know!

Out of a minor primate has developed a fabulous creature. It has two legs and walks upright and looks around it with curious eyes. It has weak hands and an insignificant brain, but it is conquering all things. Most of all, it is conquering its environment.

It has even begun speculating about me!

Seventh day—

Today there is no school.

After the pangs and labors of creation, it is fun to play again. It is like escaping the gravitational field of a white dwarf and regaining the dissipated coma.

Teacher talked to my parent again today. Teacher said I had developed remarkably in the last few days but my creation was hopelessly warped and inconsistent. Moreover, it was potentially dangerous.

Teacher said it would have to be destroyed.

My parent objected, saying that the solar phoenix reaction in the sun would lead the dangerous life-form on the third planet to develop a thermonuclear reaction of its own. With the functions I had given that life-form, the problem would take care of itself.

It wasn't my parent's responsibility, Teacher said, and Teacher couldn't take the chance.

I didn't hear who won the argument. I drifted away, feeling funny.

I don't care, really. I'm tired of the old thing anyway. I'll make a better one.

But it was the first thing I ever made, and you can't help feeling a kind of sentimental attachment.

If anyone sees a great comet plunging toward the sun, it isn't me.

Eighth day—